C

SEA CHANGE

SEA CHANGE

ROBERT B. PARKER

LARGE PRINT PRESS
An imprint of Thomson Gale, a part of The Thomson Corporation

THOMSON

™

GALE

Detroit • New York • San Francisco • New Haven, Conn. • Waterville, Maine • London

THOMSON

TM

GALE

LIBRARY OF CONGRESS CATALOGING-IN-PUBLICATION DATA

Parker, Robert B., 1932–.
  Sea change / by Robert B. Parker.
    p. cm.
  ISBN 0-7862-7370-4 (lg. print : hc : alk. paper)
    1. Stone, Jesse (Fictitious character) — Fiction. 2. Police — Massachusetts
  — Fiction. 3. Police chiefs — Fiction. 4. Massachusetts — Fiction. I. Title.
  PS3566.A686S43 2006
  813'.54—dc22
                            2006002048

ISBN 13: 978-1-59413-194-3 (sc)
Published in 2007 by arrangement with G. P. Putnam's Sons,
a division of Penguin Group (USA) Inc.

Printed in the United States of America on permanent paper
10 9 8 7 6 5 4 3 2 1

For Joan
il miglior fabbro

They were out of the harbor, off Stiles Island, in the weather. The day had turned bad. The sky was dark. The wind had gotten hard, and a thin rain slanted in front of the wind. They had drunk all the wine and talked most of the talk and now it was time to get home.

The person at the tiller said, "It feels as if there's something fouling the centerboard, could you check it?"

Florence stood and leaned over and raised the centerboard. It felt free to her. The boat slid slightly sideways. She let the board down. The boat stabilized, and came hard about, and the boom swung over the small cockpit and hit her a numbing blow in the chest and knocked the wind out of her. She pitched over the side into the black water. It was painfully cold. She went under, gasping for breath, inhaling some of the water, choking on it. She struggled toward the surface. When she broke water she could see the sailboat turning and coming back for her. She struggled to breathe, to stay afloat, to focus. In the far distance where Paradise rose up from the harbor she could see, on the top of the highest hill, the steeple of the oldest church in town. The sailboat was coming. She treaded water desperately. Only another minute at the most before the boat reached her. Hang on. Hang on. Through the gray rain, she could see the little white bone of spray at the prow, the brass turnbuckle of the mast stay, the dark protective paint on the belly of the boat, as it leaned hard to the side, straining against the wind.

In a moment it would head up into the wind and sit, its sail luffing while she got hold of the rail. She was treading water. She was afloat. She was getting her breath. The boat didn't head into the wind. It came straight on and the bow hit her in the chest and forced her under as the boat passed and sailed on. Barely conscious, she struggled to the surface. The boat was past her, sailing away. She tried to scream but she choked on the seawater. And then she went under and choked some more and lost consciousness.

Running before the wind with its sheet full out, the little sailboat headed home without her.

1

The bouncer at the Dory was holding a wet towel against his bloody nose when Jesse Stone arrived. Suitcase Simpson was with him. Simpson was in uniform. Jesse was wearing jeans and a white short-sleeved oxford shirt. His gun was on his right hip and his badge was tucked in his shirt pocket so that the shield showed.

"You usually win these, Fran," Jesse said to the bouncer.

The bouncer shrugged. His right eye was nearly closed.

"Too big for me, Jesse. You guys may have to shoot him."

"We'll see," Jesse said.

Jesse pushed into the crowded bar. There was no noise. A big man was standing on the bar drinking from a bottle of Wild Turkey. The bottle had a pour spout on it and he would hold it away from his open mouth and pour the whiskey in. The bartender, whose name was Judy, had ducked out from behind the bar and was standing near the door. She had blonde hair in a ponytail and wore sneakers, shorts and a tank top.

"You call us?" Jesse said to her.

She nodded.

"He was drunk when he came in," she said.

Jesse nodded.

"He made some remarks," Judy said. "I told him I wouldn't serve him. He made some more remarks, Fran tried to help . . ." She shrugged.

"You know who that is?" Simpson murmured in Jesse's ear.

"Carl Radborn," Jesse said. "All-Pro tackle. Shall we get his autograph?"

"Just letting you know," Simpson said.

Jesse slid through the quiet crowd with Simpson behind him.

"Hey," Radborn yelled. "Run for your fucking life, it's the Paradise cops."

Radborn was 6'5" and weighed more than 300 pounds. Standing on the bar he seemed too big for the room. Jesse smiled at him.

"Should have brought an elephant gun," Jesse said.

"Shit," Radborn said and jumped down off the bar, still holding the whiskey bottle. "You know who I am?"

"I always love that question," Jesse said. "Yeah, I know who you are. Jonathan Ogden knocked you down and stomped on your face when you played the Ravens last year."

"Fuck you," Radborn said.

"Oh," Jesse said, "I hadn't thought of it that way."

A few people snickered.

"I don't give a fuck. You a cop or what," Radborn said. "I'll kick your ass and Fat Boy's right here and now."

Simpson reddened.

"A lot of that is muscle," Jesse said.

"I play football," Radborn said. "You play football, you'll go with anybody. You ready to go?"

"Be better if you walked outside with us," Jesse said.

"Fuck you."

"I'll take that as a no," Jesse said. "Suit, gimme your stick."

Simpson took the nightstick from the loop on his belt and handed it to Jesse.

"You think that fucking toothpick gonna matter?" Radborn said.

He was six inches taller than Jesse and more than 125 pounds heavier. Jesse took the stick from Simpson and with one motion hit Radborn in the testicles with it. Radborn gasped and doubled over. Jesse stepped around him quickly and hit him behind each knee with the stick. The legs collapsed. Radborn went to his knees. Jesse took a handful of hair and yanked him forward so that he was facedown on the floor. He glanced back at Simpson.

"I played baseball," Jesse said. "Cuff him, Dan-o."

Simpson handcuffed Radborn. With help from the bouncer they got Radborn on his feet and stumbled him to the squad car and strapped him in. He'd been drinking all day. It was having its effect. He was half conscious, rocking in the backseat. He was so big that the squad car rocked with him. He bent forward suddenly against the seat belt and vomited. Some of the crowd had followed them outside. They applauded.

The two cops and the bouncer looked in at him for a moment without saying anything.

"Race Week," the bouncer said.

"And it's only the first day," Jesse said.

Simpson got in to drive and Jesse sat up front beside him. They put the front windows down. Jesse looked back through the thick wire screening that separated them from Radborn in the backseat. As he looked, Radford threw up again.

"One of the perks of being chief," Jesse said, "is you don't have to clean the patrol car."

"That be your driver's job?" Simpson said.

"Yes," Jesse said. "I believe so."

2

Jenn sat with Jesse outside, at a table on the deck of the Gray Gull restaurant, where they could look at the harbor.

"Is it always like this during Race Week?" Jenn said.

"Has been since I arrived," Jesse said.

"Just to watch a bunch of sailboats race?"

"And drink and eat and fornicate," Jesse said, "and maybe snort a little something, bet some money. Maybe make a deal with somebody important. Big boats start arriving a month before. Lot of people come here for Race Week and never see a race."

He was drinking iced tea. She had a daiquiri. She was wearing Oakley wraparounds. The veranda looked east at the harbor, and the sun was very low in the west and entirely screened from them by the body of the restaurant. Jenn was a weather girl on a Boston television station and people occasionally recognized her. The glasses didn't prevent that, and, he thought, that wasn't why she wore them.

She saw him looking at her and put her hand on top of his across the table.

"How we doing?" she said.

"So far, so good," Jesse said.

The harbor was dense with racing sailboats, and beyond, in the deeper water near the point where the harbor opened onto the limitless ocean, the big yachts lay at anchor.

"Do they race those big ones?" Jenn said.

"Some of them," Jesse said. "At the end of Race Week some of the yachts race from here to Virginia Beach. I'm told that the racing yachts are different than the yachts you just sail around in, but I'm not a sea-going guy, and I can't tell you what the difference is."

The waitress brought lobster salad for each of them and a glass of white wine for Jenn.

"It came in on the news wire that you had to arrest that huge football player yesterday," Jenn said. "One of the sports guys told me."

"He was drunk at the Dory," Jesse said. "Broke the bouncer's nose."

"The sports guy said you subdued him with a nightstick."

"I borrowed Suit's," Jesse said.

"I was with, what's his name, Redford?"

"Radborn," Jesse said.

"I was with Radborn at a charity thing," Jenn said. "He's enormous. Weren't you intimidated? Even a little?"

"The bigger they are . . ." Jesse said.

"Oh God," Jenn said. "Not that."

Jesse smiled. "How about, 'it's not the size of the dog in the fight . . .'?"

"I'm serious. It interests me. You interest me."

"If you've been a cop," Jesse said, "especially a big city cop, like I was, after awhile you sort of expect to handle it."

"But he's twice your size."

"It's not really about the other guy," Jesse said. "It's about yourself."

"So what's your secret?"

Jesse grinned.

"Usually it's backup."

"And this time?"

"Well, Suit was there, but the guy was out of control and the place was crowded . . ."

"And he gave you attitude," Jenn said.

"He did. So if you're going to go, do it quick. You gotta get a guy like Radford right away or you're going to have to shoot him."

"What did you do?"

"I hit him in the balls with Suit's stick."

15

"Ouch," Jenn said. "And that was it?"

"Essentially it was," Jesse said.

"I was talking to the bartender before you arrived," Jenn said.

"Doc," Jesse said.

"Yes, he said you didn't press charges."

Jesse drank some iced tea, and grinned at her as he put the glass down.

"This morning when he was sober with a deadly hangover, we gave him the choice: district court or clean the squad car."

"Clean the squad car?"

"He puked in it."

"Oh yuck," Jenn said. "So much for dinner."

"Don't kid me, you're about as queasy as a buzzard."

"But much cuter," Jenn said. "Did he do it?"

"He did," Jesse said. "And we let him walk."

"With his hangover," Jenn said.

"Awful one, as far as I could tell."

"You would know about those," Jenn said.

"I would."

They ate their lobster salad for a time. It was mediocre. Jesse always thought the food at the Gray Gull was mediocre, but it was a handy place, and friendly, and had a

16

great view of the harbor on a summer night sitting on the deck. Jesse didn't care much what he ate anyway.

When they finished supper they walked along the waterfront for a stretch. The street were full of people, many of them drunk, some of them raucous. Jesse seemed not to notice them.

"I brought my stuff," Jenn said.

"For an overnight?"

"Yes," Jenn said. "I'm not on air until tomorrow afternoon."

"You bring it in the house?"

"Yes, I unpacked in the bedroom."

"That sounds promising," Jesse said.

"It is promising, but I need to walk off my supper first."

"You never were a love-on-a-full-stomach girl," Jesse said.

"I like things just right," Jenn said.

"Sure," Jesse said.

Away from the wharf the street life grew sparse. No more bars and restaurants, simply the old houses pressed up against the sidewalks. There were narrow streets, and brick sidewalks, bird's-eye glass windows, weathered siding, and widow's walks and weathervanes. It was dark and there weren't many streetlights. Away from the Race Week crowds, the old town was dim

17

and European. Jenn took Jesse's hand as they walked.

"This time," Jenn said, "things might be just right."

"Maybe," Jesse said. "If we're careful."

The street-side windows were lighted in many of the homes, and people sat, watching television, or reading something, or talking with someone, or drinking alone, behind the drawn curtains only inches away from Jesse and Jenn as they walked.

"How long since you've had a drink, Jesse?"

"Ten months and thirteen days," Jesse said.

"Miss it?"

"Yes."

"Maybe, in time, you'll get to where you can have a drink occasionally," Jenn said. "You know, socially."

"Maybe," Jesse said.

"Maybe in awhile you and I can be more than, you know, one day at a time."

"Maybe," Jesse said.

In this neighborhood fewer lights were on. The streets seemed darker. Their footsteps were very clear in the silent sea-smelling air.

"You've slept with a lot of women, since we got divorced," Jenn said.

Jesse smiled in the darkness.

"No such thing as too many," he said.

"There certainly is," Jenn said, "and you know it."

"I do know it."

"There's been a lot of men," Jenn said. "For me."

"Yes."

"Does that bother you?"

"Yes."

"Do you want to talk about it?"

Jesse shook his head.

"No," he said. "Not yet."

"Not yet?"

"Not until I understand it more."

Jenn nodded.

"Do you still talk to Dix?"

"Sometimes."

"Do you talk about that?"

"Sometimes," Jesse said. "The women in my life bother you?"

"Not very much," Jenn said. "Mostly I don't think about them."

In their walk they had made a slow loop along the waterfront, up into the town, and back around down to the waterfront again to Jesse's condominium. They stopped at Jesse's front steps.

"Well," Jenn said. "You are the man in my life now."

"Yes," Jesse said.

"You want to neck on the porch for a while?" Jenn said. "Or go right on in and get serious?"

Jesse put his arms around her.

"No hurry," he said.

"I love that in a man," Jenn whispered, and put her face up and kissed him.

3

The body moved gently, facedown, against the town dock, in the dark faintly oily water, among the broken crab shells, dead fish and fragments of Styrofoam which seemed to survive all adversity. It tossed easily on the small rounded swells of a powerboat wake. The seagulls were interested in the body, and below Jesse could see the shimmer of small fish.

Simpson said, "A woman, I think, wearing a dress."

"Not proof positive, but we'll assume," Jesse said.

They looked at her as she eddied in the seaweed, and the body turned slightly so that the feet swung toward shore.

"Gotta get her out," Jesse said.

"She been in awhile," Simpson said. "You can see the bloat from here."

"Get a tarp," Jesse said, "and you and Arthur and Peter Perkins get her up on the dock and put the tarp over her. Don't want the sailors all puking before the race."

"What about the cops?" Simpson said.

"Try not to," Jesse said. "Bad for the department image."

Jesse had seen enough floaters, and he had no need to see another one. Nor smell one. He looked at the small racing boats forming up and heading out to the harbor mouth where they would race off Stiles Island. Out by the end of Stiles Island he could see whitecaps. Be some bumpy races today. Behind him the coroner's wagon arrived and the ME's people got out a gurney and wheeled it down the ramp to the dock. One of them, a woman, squatted on her heels over the body and pulled back the canvas. Jesse saw all three of his cops look away. He smiled. The ME woman didn't seem bothered, holding up the tarp, inspecting the body. When she was through she put the tarp back and jerked her thumb toward the wagon and they got the body on the gurney, and wheeled it up to the truck. A small crowd, mostly teenaged kids, watched the process. Occasionally one of them would giggle nervously.

"Anything interesting," Jesse said to the woman.

"Need to get her on the table," she said. "She's too big a mess to tell much here."

"ID?" Jesse said.

"Not yet."

"She in the water long?"

"Yes," the woman said. "Looks like the crabs been at her."

"Crabs?"

"Un-huh."

"Means she was on the bottom," Jesse said.

"Or at the water's edge."

Jesse nodded. "Anything else?" he said.

She shook her head.

"We'll know more after we get her into the shop," she said.

"Mind if I send my evidence specialist along with you?" Jesse said.

"Hell no," the woman smiled, "we'll show him some stuff."

"Oh, Jesus," Peter Perkins said.

Simpson watched the van pull away. He was very fair, with a round face and pink cheeks. Now there was no pink.

"You see something like that," Simpson said, "chewed up, full of bloat, and stinking, makes you wonder about life and death, you know?"

Jesse nodded.

"I mean," Simpson said, "it's hard to imagine something like that going to heaven."

"The body don't go, anyway," Arthur said.

"Yeah, I know."

The three men didn't say anything.

"You ever think about stuff like that, Jesse?" Simpson said.

Jesse nodded.

"So whaddya think?"

Jesse smiled.

"I think I don't know," he said.

"That's it?" Simpson said.

"Yeah," Jesse said. *"I don't know* doesn't mean there's no afterlife. Doesn't mean there is. Means, *I don't know."*

"That enough for you, Jesse?"

"Kind of has to be. Universe is too big and complicated for me to understand."

"That's where faith comes in," Arthur said.

"If it can," Jesse said.

"Can for me," Arthur said.

Jesse nodded.

"Whatever works," he said. "Let's see if we can find out who our floater was."

4

Jesse was leaning on the front desk in Paradise Police Headquarters reading the ME's report on the floater. Molly was working the phones. It was only 8:40 in the morning and the phones were quiet.

"You think she came off one of the yachts?" Molly said.

Jesse smiled. Molly always looked too small for the gun belt. In fact there wasn't all that much that Molly was too small for. She was dark-haired and cute, full of curiosity and absolute resolve.

"Only if they got here before Race Week," Jesse said. "ME says she's been in the water awhile."

"Any signs of trauma?"

"Nope, but it's pretty hard to tell. Crab, ah, markings indicate she was probably on the bottom, which might suggest she was weighted, and decomposition, tidal movement, whatever, pulled her loose and sent her up. Or she could just have been in shallow water."

"Could be lobster markings," Molly said.

"I'll keep it in mind," Jesse said. "Next time I'm ordering dinner at the Gray Gull."

He heard himself say Gray Gull the way locals did, as if it were one word, with the stress on *gray*, not *gull*. *I been here awhile,* Jesse thought. *I'm beginning to be local.*

"It couldn't be gulls?" Molly said.

"No."

"How do they know?"

"They know," Jesse said. "There's evidence of blunt trauma on her body, but nothing that couldn't have come from being rolled against rocks by the surf."

"Oh. Well if she did come off a yacht, it's strange no one has reported her missing."

"No one seems to have reported her missing, yacht or no yacht," Jesse said.

"We got five missing persons in the Northeast that could be her," Molly said. "Except none of the dental IDs match."

Jesse wore blue jeans and sneakers and a short-sleeved white police chief shirt, with the badge pinned to the shirt pocket. He carried the snub-nosed .38 that he'd brought with him from L.A. The issue gun, a nine-millimeter semiautomatic, she knew, was in the right-hand bottom drawer of his desk. His hair was cut short. He was tanned, and, Molly always noticed this about him, while he wasn't a particularly big man he seemed very strong, as if his center were muscular.

The phone rang and Molly took it and said, "Yes ma'am. We'll have someone check right on it." She wrote nothing down, and when she hung up she took no further action.

"Mrs. Billups?" Jesse said.

Molly nodded.

"Says there's a man she doesn't recognize walking past her house. He looks sinister."

"How many is that so far this month?"

"Four," Molly said.

"And this year?"

"Oh God," Molly said, "infinity."

"Mrs. Billups hasn't got much else to occupy her," Jesse said. "Who's on patrol?"

"Suit."

"Have him drive slowly past her house," Jesse said.

"There's nothing there, Jesse."

"I know, and you know. But Mrs. Billups doesn't know."

"You are awful tenderhearted," Molly said, "for a guy who banged Carl Radborn in the balls with a stick."

"She'll peek out the window when she sees the patrol car," Jesse said. "Have Suit

27

give her a little wave. Maybe a thumbs-up."

Molly shook her head in slow disapproval, but she turned as she did so, and called Simpson on the radio.

"Go do another Mrs. Billups drive-by," she said.

"Oh shit, Molly, that old biddy sees things every day."

Jesse leaned into the microphone.

He said, "Serve and protect, Suit."

There was silence for a minute, then Simpson said, "Aye, aye, skipper."

Jesse went into the squad room in back and got two coffees and brought one in for Molly.

"If you're missing from a town or a city, people might not notice right away," Jesse said. "But a yacht?"

"So she's probably not off one of the yachts."

"Or, if she is, people don't wish it known," Jesse said.

"Which would mean that someone murdered her."

"Or that someone doesn't want anyone to know she was on the yacht."

Molly nodded.

"Like somebody else's wife," she said.

"Or a hooker, or a juror in a pending

civil trial, or something neither of us can think of."

"There's nothing neither of us can think of," Molly said.

"Except who the floater is."

"ME can't give you anything?"

"Sure they can," Jesse said.

He looked at the ME's initial report.

"Floater was about thirty-five. Alive she was about five-seven, probably weighed a hundred and thirty pounds. Brown eyes, natural brunette. She was wearing an expensive dress and silk underwear when she died. She had been drinking. She showed traces of cocaine, and she was a smoker. Her breasts had been enhanced. She was alive when she went in the water. She was not a virgin."

"No kidding."

"Just running down the list, Moll," Jesse said. "She had never had children."

"We could start checking with plastic surgeons," Molly said. "See if any enhancement patients are missing."

"If it were done by a plastic surgeon," Jesse said. "Any MD can do this kind of surgery."

"But most intelligent people wouldn't go to an allergist or somebody," Molly said. "Would you?"

"For breast enhancement?" Jesse said.

"You know what I mean," Molly said.

Another call came in. Molly answered and listened and wrote down an address.

"Okay, Mr. Bradley," she said. "I'll have an officer there in a few minutes. Call back if there's any problem. And stay away from the animal."

"Rabid animal?" Jesse said.

"Skunk. Guy working on a roof up on Sterling Circle says it's staggering and walking in circles in the street. He was on his cell phone."

"Suit should have saved Mrs. Billups by now. Have him go up and shoot the skunk."

"What if it's not really rabid?" Molly said.

"Family can sue us."

Molly called Simpson. When she was through she turned back to Jesse.

"Do people like urologists really do plastic surgery?"

"They may legally do so," Jesse said. "Some people don't know one doctor from another. In the white coat they all look the same."

"A woman wearing silk underwear would know," Molly said.

Jesse grinned.

"Depends who bought the underwear," he said.

"Still, odds are it would be a plastic surgeon. I can make some calls."

"Sure," Jesse said. "If we're lucky, maybe she did them around here."

"Of course," Molly said. "She could have driven here from Grand Junction, Colorado, and parked on the Neck someplace and jumped in."

"Except we haven't found any abandoned vehicles," Jesse said.

"Or someone was with her and threw her in and drove away."

"Or she's a space alien," Jesse said.

"Or, just shut up," Molly said.

"I am the chief law enforcement officer of Paradise, Massachusetts," Jesse said. "And your chief. Surely you can be more respectful than that."

"Of course," Molly said. "I'm sorry . . . shut up, sir."

"Thank you."

"Are they all through with her?" Molly said.

"The coroner? No, this is a preliminary report. They're still poking around."

"Ick," Molly said.

"Cops don't say 'ick.' "

Molly laughed and leaned over the desk

and kissed Jesse on the forehead.

"Do cops do that?" Molly said.

"Oh yeah," Jesse said, "most of them."

The phone rang again and Molly answered, "Paradise Police," while Jesse took the coroner's report back to his office.

5

Dix always looked so clean, Jesse thought. His white shirts were always brilliant white. His head gleamed as if he had just shaved it, and his face glistened with aftershave.

"Jenn asked me the other day if it bothered me about her being with other men."

Dix nodded. He sat with his elbows on the arms of his chair, his hands clasped chest high. They were big square competent hands.

"I said it did."

"You wanna talk about that?" Dix said.

"Yes."

"Whaddya want to say?"

"I, well, I mean I hate it," Jesse said. "But that doesn't seem too weird."

"Hate it that she was with other men?"

"Them having sex," Jesse said.

Dix nodded. Neither of them said anything. Dix's desk was completely empty except for a phone and a calendar pad. His degrees were on the wall, and there was a couch, which Jesse had never used, against the wall behind him.

"Does it bother you to think of them talking intimately, laughing together, sharing a joke, enjoying a meal, watching a ball game?"

"Sure. Isn't it, to use a nice shrink word, *appropriate,* to be jealous when your wife's cheating on you?" Jesse said.

"It is certainly human," Dix said. "Is it with the same intensity that you think of her having sex?"

"No."

"Is she cheating on you now?"

"No. Right now we're good."

"So?" Dix said.

Jesse started to speak and stopped and sat. Dix was quiet.

"I can't seem to let it go," Jesse said.

"What part can't you let go of?" Dix said.

"Her having sex. I think about it. I imagine it. I can't get rid of it when I'm with her."

Dix waited, his head cocked slightly. Jesse was staring at his hands, which were clasped in front of him. After a time he looked up at Dix.

"It's like, almost, like I maybe don't want to let it go."

Dix's face changed just enough for Jesse to see that he approved of the direction the

34

conversation was taking.

"What the hell do I get out of it?" Jesse said.

"Something," Dix said. "Or you'd let it go."

"Yes."

Again they were silent. The hushed whir of the air conditioning was the only sound in the office. It was hard to imagine Dix being hot, or tired, or puzzled, Jesse thought. No one could put up with silence like Dix could. It was like his natural element. Jesse felt winded. He took in another big breath.

"You went out with a lot of other women after your separation and divorce," Dix said.

"Sure."

"Did you imagine them with other men?"

"Not really," Jesse said. "I love Jenn. I liked everyone I slept with. But I never loved them the way I love Jenn."

"Therefore?" Dix said.

"Therefore I didn't care who else they'd slept with," Jesse said.

"Excuse the cliché," Dix said. "But isn't that more about you, about how you felt, than it is about Jenn or the other women?"

Jesse looked blankly at Dix for a moment.

"What the hell is wrong with me?" Jesse said.

"You're human," Dix said. "A common ailment."

6

When Jesse got back to the station Jenn was in his office, sitting at his desk with the swivel chair tilted back, her legs crossed under her short skirt, showing a lot of thigh. Jesse felt the little pinch of desire in his stomach. He always felt it when he saw her. It was so consistently a part of being with her that he just thought of it as part of the nature of things. He had always assumed it was what everyone felt when they looked at the person they loved. Why worry about it now? Was he looking for something to worry about?

"Oh Jesse," she said. "I have great news. They're doing an hour-long special at the station on Race Week. And I'm going to be the on-camera host and do the voiceover, too."

"Wow," Jesse said.

"It's not just some feature for the six o'clock news," she said. "It's a full-hour feature and the company plans to syndicate it."

"That's great, Jenn."

"I'll be here every day with the crew. I'll have input. Jesse, this is a really big break for me. We're owned by Allied Broadcasting, and they have stations in most of the major markets."

Jesse went around the desk and bent over and kissed her. She put her arms around his neck, kept her mouth pressed against his and let him pull her from the chair when he straightened up. They held the kiss a long time. When they broke, Jesse exhaled audibly.

"When's it being broadcast?" he said.

"Well, in syndication it varies by market. But we're hoping to show it next year around Race Week," Jenn said.

Jenn kept her arms around his neck and her body pressed against him.

"So you have a whole year to edit and do whatever you do," Jesse said.

"Yes. Lay in the narration, the music track, enhance the pictures, spruce up the sound. A lot of work, and it gives you an idea of how much hope they have for this, that they'd give us so much time."

"A year," Jesse said.

He felt the press of her thighs against him, of her breasts. He felt the miasmic press of emotion that he always felt.

"Not really a year. They need it finished in December for the syndication deal."

"Still a lot better than editing this afternoon for on air tonight," Jesse said.

They let go of each other.

"Here," Jenn said. "Sit in your chair. I just couldn't wait to tell."

Jesse sat behind his desk. Jenn took a chair on the other side.

"You need a place to stay up here?" Jesse said.

"When we worked late, I was hoping to bunk in with you."

"That'll work," Jesse said.

Here was something to worry about.

"I know you're not so sure you want to live together full time," Jenn said.

"I'm not sure what I want," Jesse said. "Except you . . . exclusively."

She nodded.

"Well, I won't be here every night," Jenn said.

"One night at a time," Jesse said, and smiled. "They know you used to be married to the chief of police?"

"I think so. Truth is, I think it's one reason I got the job. They figure it'll give me extra access. I mean I'm a fucking weather girl, you know?"

"People like you, Jenn."

"As long as you do," Jenn said.

"I love you."

"Does that mean you really, really like me?"

"I think so," Jesse said.

7

Arthur Angstrom came into Jesse's office with a leathery gray-haired man that Jesse didn't know.

"This is Mr. Guilfoyle," Arthur said. "Runs a small boat rental operation out of Ned's Cove. Says one of his boats is missing. Don't seem like much, except for that floater, so . . ." He shrugged.

Jesse nodded.

"Thanks, Arthur," Jesse said. "Have a seat, Mr. Guilfoyle. Tell me about your boat."

"A little day sailor, twelve feet long. Marconi rigged, no jib. Centerboard."

Jesse nodded as if he understood, or cared.

"And when did it go missing."

"Woman rented it from me last month," Guilfoyle said. "Never returned it."

"How long did she rent it for?"

"Just the day. These boats sleep no one, you know? Nobody rents them overnight."

"Do you have the woman's name?" Jesse said.

"Sure," Guilfoyle said. "I don't pass

these things out like samples. I got a credit card and a driver's license. But the thing is, my boat is down in Nelson's place. In among the other boats. Nelson didn't even know he had it, until one of the kids that works for him tried to put one of his own boats away and there was a boat in the slot. He recognized my ID number on the bow and called me. For crissake, she didn't even clean it out."

"What was in it?"

"Trash. Half a loaf of bread, some plastic cups, paper napkins all soaking wet, some moldy cheese, couple apple cores, empty wine bottle, some rotten grapes. Didn't even put it in the damn bag."

"Where was the bag from?"

"Ranch Market, in town. Like somebody bought stuff for a picnic."

"Just lying on the floor of the boat," Jesse said.

"Yeah."

"Who's Nelson," Jesse said.

"Paradise Rentals," Guilfoyle said. "He's the big guy in the business, right over here off the town wharf."

Jesse nodded.

"I know the place. You think she made a mistake, took it back to the wrong place?"

"How do you do that?" Guilfoyle said.

He wore a pink striped shirt and white duck trousers with wide red suspenders. The shirt was unbuttoned over his chest, as if he were proud of the gray hair.

"I mean he's here, I'm way the hell down the other end of the harbor. He's got a hundred boats. I got fifteen. He's short and fat."

"And you look like Cesar Romero," Jesse said.

"Yeah, right. So how does somebody make that kind of mistake."

"Hard to figure," Jesse said.

"Plus I got her damn driver's license. I always hold it until they bring the boat back."

"You have that with you?" Jesse said.

"Yeah. The credit card slip and her license."

Guilfoyle took a brown envelope out of his hip pocket and put it on the desk in front of Jesse.

"Kid's sailing the boat over to my place. I got to charge her credit card for all the time it's been gone, you know."

"That'll be up to you and the credit card company," Jesse said. "I'll need to hang on to the license for a few days."

"What if they want some kind of proof?"

"I'll make it available," Jesse said. "I just want to see what happened to the woman."

41

"Something happened?"

"Yep."

"I don't want to get involved in no trouble," Guilfoyle said.

"Don't blame you," Jesse said.

"But you think I might?"

"Not unless you're what happened to her," Jesse said.

"It's that dead girl they found floating down by the wharf."

"Don't know if it is or not," Jesse said.

"But if you look at the picture on her driver's license . . ." Guilfoyle paused.

Jesse was shaking his head.

"Oh," Guilfoyle said.

"Thanks for coming in, Mr. Guilfoyle."

"Yeah, well, I don't want no trouble over this. I just want to get paid for the time my boat was missing."

"And I wish you well on that," Jesse said.

"I'm going to talk with a lawyer."

"That'll be swell," Jesse said.

Guilfoyle looked at him. Jesse looked back.

"Don't lose that license, either," Guilfoyle said.

"Okay," Jesse said.

Guilfoyle lingered.

"Thanks for stopping by," Jesse said.

Guilfoyle hesitated another moment, then went.

8

It was a Florida driver's license. The photo was not flattering. But it showed that she was blond and thirtyish. *Kind of cheap-looking,* Jesse thought, and smiled. It was something his mother would have said. *What the hell does it even mean? Mostly a matter of hair and makeup, probably.* Her name was Florence E. Horvath. Her address was in Fort Lauderdale. Her date of birth was February 13, 1970. Jesse took the license and credit card to the copy machine, made a copy of each and took the copies to the front desk and gave them to Molly.

"Call Fort Lauderdale," Jesse said. "Tell them we have a body that might be this woman, see what they got on her, or what they can get. Dental records would be good. Then call the bank that issued this credit card and see what you can get — history of purchases this month and so forth."

"I know you'll explain this to me later," Molly said.

"Being chief means never having to explain," Jesse said.

"Might mean making your own coffee every morning, too," Molly said.

"I'll explain this to you later," Jesse said.

Molly turned to the switchboard. Jesse went back to his office and looked in the phone book. There was only one Horvath listed in Paradise. He called. There was no one there named Florence, nor did they know anyone named Florence. He called the Florida Department of Highway Safety and Motor Vehicles, waded through a long menu of options, finally got someone in enforcement and arranged to have some blowups of Florence Horvath's driver's license photograph sent to Paradise. The he got up and went into the squad room where Peter Perkins was drinking a Diet Pepsi and reading the *Globe* sports section.

"You get through with the sports page," Jesse said, "see if you can scan this license picture into the computer and send it over to Forensics. Ask them if it could be the floater."

"Condition of the body," Perkins said, "I don't think they can tell much."

"Ask them if anything here rules Florence out."

"Okay, Jess," Perkins said and folded the

paper and put it on the conference table. "You're the chief."

"Yes I am," Jesse said.

In the hall outside the squad room he saw Suitcase Simpson come in herding three college-aged kids, all of whom were drunk.

"I want a lawyah," a blond kid kept saying. "I got right to a lawyah."

"What's up," Jesse said. "A riot in day care?"

"They were pissing in the watering trough in the town common," Simpson said.

"Put them in a cell," Jesse said, "and call their parents to come get them."

One of the kids was wearing plaid shorts and a muscle shirt he was too skinny to sustain.

"What charge," he said. "Can't lock us with no charge."

"Inadequate potty training," Jesse said. "Go on down there with Officer Simpson, and when you get sick try to puke in the hopper."

Simpson herded them ahead of him toward the cell corridor. They were saying they weren't drunk. There was no need to call their parents. They were being picked on for being kids. This was harassment. There was a mention of police brutality, then the door to the cell corridor closed and shut it off.

As Jesse walked past the desk, Molly said, "Fort Lauderdale says they'll send a patrol car over to check on the address, and they'll see what they can find on her. Like who her dentist is, or was. Bank will send us a copy of her last statement, and a printout of the credit card charges for the period since the statement."

"Thank you," Jesse said. "You ever piss in a watering trough?"

"That what Suit busted them for?"

"Yep."

"I am a mother and a wife, and an Irish Catholic," Molly said. "I don't piss at all."

9

They were eating pepper and mushroom pizza at the little table on Jesse's balcony, with the strong salt sea smell of the harbor drifting pleasantly around them on the soft July air. Jenn had a glass of red wine. Jesse was drinking a Coke.

"When we're together," Jesse said, "what do you feel coming from me."

"I feel strong vibes that I should undress and lie down," Jenn said.

"Really?"

Jenn was about to bite the point off a pizza slice. She stopped and looked at him with the pizza poised in front of her.

"You're serious, aren't you," she said.

"Yes."

Jenn put the pizza slice back on the plate.

"Well, I . . . you know I don't think much about stuff like that," she said.

"I been talking with Dix about it," Jesse said. "I need help with it."

"Well, I mean, I know you love me."

"Yes."

"And I love you," Jenn said.

"Perfect," Jesse said.

"We've been together for a long time," Jenn said.

"Sort of," Jesse said.

"I mean, even at our worst and most separate we were connected."

"Yes," Jesse said.

"And we are more than two people who fuck."

"Yes," Jesse said.

"Which," Jenn said, "is much better than being two people who don't."

"So you don't mind about the undressing and lying down."

"I like it," Jenn said.

"And you don't feel objectified."

"Ob— what?" Jenn said. "Christ, you're getting like whatsisname, Hamlet. You think too much. We are much more than the damn missionary position and we both know it."

"And there's nothing wrong with the missionary position," Jesse said.

"A little unimaginative, maybe," Jenn said.

In the harbor there were lights showing on the bigger boats moored farther out. Cocktail on the deck, supper cooking in the galley, the running lights of a small tender boat creeping soundlessly across the black water like a firefly. Jesse drank some Coke. Caffeine. *Any stimulus is better than none.*

"Dix and I talked about how sexually charged our relationship is," Jesse said.

"And that's a bad thing?" Jenn said.

She poured herself a half glass more of red wine.

"Maybe you're supposed to sexualize our relationship. Ever think about that, Hamlet boy? Maybe it has to do with you loving me more than the spoken word can tell."

"Well," Jesse said, "there's that."

10

Healy hiked his pants up at the knee when he sat, to keep the crease. He had on a tan poplin suit and a coffee-colored snap-brim straw hat with a wide brown headband. His plain-toed cordovan shoes gleamed with polish.

"On my way home," Healy said. "Thought I'd stop in, see what's happening with your floater."

Jesse pointed over his shoulder at the photo.

"That her?" Healy said.

A blowup of Florence Horvath's driver's license was stuck on a cork board to the left of the window behind Jesse's desk.

"That's her, Captain," Jesse said. "Florence Horvath, thirty-four years old, address in Fort Lauderdale. She had her teeth cleaned a month ago and charged it on her credit card. We called the dentist, got the dental records, forensic people compared them."

"You're lucky," Healy said. "Lot of floaters are such a mess we never do figure out who they are."

"Got nothing to do with luck," Jesse said.

"Right," Healy said. "It was crack police work that some guy walked in and handed you her driver's license and credit card."

"And," Jesse said, "we didn't lose them."

"Got me there," Healy said. "Now that you know who she is, do you know why she's up here?"

"Not yet."

"I'm only a state police captain," Healy said, "not a chief of police, like you, but since you found her in the water and since this is Race Week, could there be a connection?"

"I got a couple of people checking the yachts in the harbor, see if any of them are out of Fort Lauderdale."

"Or even docked there in the last three weeks," Healy said.

"If she came on a yacht."

"If," Healy said. "How about the airlines?"

"No Florence Horvath on any of them."

"Not just from Florida," Healy said.

"From anywhere," Jesse said.

"Molly been working her ass off," Healy said. "How about a car."

"Nope."

"Rental car?"

"None of the big agencies, at least, have her in the computer," Jesse said. "We haven't gotten to the Rent-a-Lemon yet."

"Nothing on her credit card to indicate a rental."

"Could have several credit cards."

"True."

"Hotels?" Healy said.

"What is this," Jesse said, "a quiz?"

"Trying to learn police work," Healy said.

"She's not registered in any of the area hotels."

"Including Boston?"

"Including Boston."

"Anybody in town she might be visiting?" Healy said.

"One family named Horvath. I called them. They never heard of her."

"Doesn't mean they didn't kill her."

"We don't know if anyone killed her," Jesse said. "Could just as well be an accident for all the forensics we got."

"Sure," Healy said. "She fell overboard and drowned and no one noticed."

"For all we know," Jesse said, "she fell off the *Queen Elizabeth* on her way to Liverpool and the currents brought her in."

"You think so?" Healy said.

"No," Jesse said.

"Usually when someone is missing for the length of time she was in the water," Healy said, "somebody wonders where she is."

"That's true whether it's murder or not," Jesse said.

"But if she were traveling, and the only person who knew her was the person she was traveling with, and that person killed her . . ." Healy rolled his hand.

Jesse leaned back in his swivel chair and grinned at Healy.

"It was a quiz, and we both aced it," Jesse said. "Sure, I'm with you. I think she was murdered."

"But you have no proof," Healy said.

"Hell no," Jesse said. "Not yet."

"She might have arrived by bus," Healy said.

"Yeah, and she might have hitchhiked. I got twelve people in this department including me. We're dancing as fast as we can dance."

Healy smiled.

"You got a homicide. I'm the commanding officer of the state homicide unit."

"So you're offering to help?"

"I am."

"Never too big to give the little guy a hand," Jesse said.

"Exactly," Healy said.

"Just as long as we're clear on whose case it is."

"It belongs to all of us," Healy said, "who love truth and justice."

"Like hell," Jesse said. "It belongs to me."

"Oh," Healy said. He shrugged. "Okay."

11

Jesse was on the phone to a detective in Fort Lauderdale named Kelly Cruz.

"Your floater was a woman of means," Kelly Cruz said.

"Really?"

"Un-huh, family owns a bunch of health food markets all over the South. Plum and Partridge."

"Cute," Jesse said.

"It's even cuter," Kelly Cruz said. "Family name is Plum."

"Not Horvath," Jesse said.

"Nope, that's a married name," Kelly Cruz said. "She's had several."

"You know the husbands?" Jesse said.

"Not yet," Kelly Cruz said. "But she was divorced most recently from a guy named Lawton Horvath."

"What do you know about Lawton?"

"White, blond hair, even tan, slim, good at golf and tennis, pretty good at bridge, no visible means of support."

"When's the last time Lawton saw her?" Jesse said.

"When they got divorced. He got the house and a cash settlement. She moved here."

"Worked out nicely for Lawton," Jesse said. "He with anyone now?"

He could hear the laughter in Kelly Cruz's voice.

"Attractive young heiress, recently divorced, with a thing for older men," she said.

"We may have stumbled across his means of support," Jesse said.

"We're law officers," Kelly Cruz said. "We're probably too suspicious."

"What else you know about Florence?"

"Soon as she moved to Fort Lauderdale she joined the East Bay Yacht Club," Kelly Cruz said. "Started hanging out at the bar there. Bartender says she was making a lot of friends fast."

"Male friends?"

"Yep."

"Got any names?"

"Not yet, you know, it's not really our case," Kelly Cruz said. "I'm the only one working it."

"Understand," Jesse said.

"I found something sort of interesting when I tossed her condo. I'll FedEx it to you, you gimme a FedEx number."

"Tight budget in Fort Lauderdale," Jesse said.

"Like I say, it's not our case."

Jesse gave her the Federal Express number.

"What are you going to send me?" he said.

"Videotape. Florence and two guys having sex together."

"Amateur?" Jesse said.

"Far as I can tell. She's having sex with both of them at the same time," Kelly Cruz said. "Looks uncomfortable as hell to me but she seemed happy with it. Kept turning to smile into the camera. Sort of proud."

"As well she should be," Jesse said. "You got anything else?"

"I got a call into her family but so far nothing back. I'm working on the earlier husbands, but so far no names. She used to live in Boca. I'll check around up there. Not too many people knew much about her around here."

"It's ten or fifteen miles, isn't it?" Jesse said. "You sure the budget will stand it?"

"Good, be a northern wiseass," Kelly Cruz said. "It encourages us down here in the swamps."

"Just a little light-hearted banter," Jesse said.

"Is that what it was," Kelly Cruz said.

"You hotshots learn anything up there?"

"We're in the middle of a series of yacht races up here," Jesse said. "Race Week."

"Oh boy," Kelly Cruz said.

"Three of the yachts are out of Fort Lauderdale," Jesse said.

"Hot damn," Kelly Cruz said. "I'm only a detective for five years, but that might be a clue."

"Might be," Jesse said. "They are owned by the following, you got a pencil?"

"I'm ready."

"Thomas Ralston," Jesse said. "Allan Pinkton. Harold Berger."

"Addresses?"

"All in Fort Lauderdale," Jesse said and read them off.

"Never heard of any of them," Kelly Cruz said. "But they probably never heard of me, either. I'll check them out. They may not be home, of course, they may be up there taking part in the excitement."

"You seem negative, Detective Cruz," Jesse said, "about yacht racing."

"Don't mean to," Kelly Cruz said. "Must be at least as exciting as watching a miniature golf match."

Jesse was silent for a moment.

"Well, no," Jesse said slowly. "It's not that much fun."

12

Channel 3 Action News set up downtown in Paradise, in the parking lot behind the Ranch Market. There was an equipment truck, and an air-conditioned mobile home to house production, wardrobe, and makeup and Jenn. Jenn had a small dressing room in it, with her own bathroom. A maze of hookups ran around the trailer and across the parking lot.

"I can even take a shower," Jenn said.

"Always wise," Jesse said.

A stocky strong-looking woman came in without knocking. She had short gray hair and Oakley sunglasses and seemed, even standing still, to be in a hurry.

"Marty," Jenn said, "this is my . . . friend Jesse Stone. He's the police chief here. Jesse, this is Marty Freeman, my producer."

"Stone?" Marty said. "Same name as yours."

"We used to be married," Jenn said.

"Nice to meet you," Marty said. "Come on, Jenn, got to use all the light we can."

Jenn was in full makeup. She kissed Jesse, very carefully, on the mouth, and went out after Marty. Jesse watched as she went away. She had on a dark blue top and white pants, and expensive sneakers. Very yacht-y. The pants fit her well, and Jesse watched her backside twitch as she walked away. He was seeing her sexually again. Was he supposed to? Christ, who wouldn't see her sexually? He looked around the small dressing room. There was a small closet with several changes of clothes. He could smell her perfume. He knew that when she took a shower and toweled off, she would spray scent in the air and walk into it naked. He wondered how many other men knew that. He imagined them watching her, as he had. A group of them. Faceless, nameless, somehow triumphant. Laughing and elbowing each other like players in a bad farce. She smiled at them. Soon she'd have sex with them. He could hear himself breathing. *That's it,* he thought. *That's the bastard. I don't know what it is yet, but it's not love.*

He looked at himself in the mirror. His face looked ordinary, the way it always looked. He spoke to the image in the mirror.

"Man," he heard himself say. "I need a drink."

60

13

"Everybody's in the squad room," Molly said. "Alert and ready to examine evidence."

"Video come in from Fort Lauderdale?" Jesse said.

"How'd you guess?"

"Male intuition," Jesse said. "Who's in the cars?"

"Martin and Friedman," Molly said. "Not happy."

"And the other eight members of Paradise's finest?"

"In the squad room," Molly said. "Waiting for you. Probably sent out for popcorn."

"You want to watch it?"

"I'm a cop," Molly said. "I need to see it, I'll see it."

"You don't need to see it with eight lecherous loudmouths," Jesse said. "Stay on the desk. There's something you need to see, you can watch it alone later."

Molly was silent for a moment.

"I'm part of the department, Jesse," Molly said softly. "I don't want everyone else to know something I don't know."

Jesse said, "Somebody has to be on the desk, Moll."

She nodded. Jesse turned toward the squad room.

"I'll watch it later," Molly said.

"Absolutely," Jesse said. "You can use the VCR in my office."

Molly was silent for another moment. Then, just as Jesse was opening the door to the squad room, she said, "Thank you."

Jesse said, "You're welcome," and went in.

The cops were gathered at the long table. The VCR and monitor, which were on a small metal cart, had been wheeled into position at the foot of the table. The screen was glowing. Jesse's chair at the head of the table was empty, and in front of it was the padded mailer from Kelly Cruz. All of the cops were drinking coffee and someone had brought a cup for Jesse. He peeled the lid off as he sat down.

"No Jujubes?" Jesse said.

"We was going to get a keg of beer," Suitcase Simpson said. "But we figured you'd be prudish about it."

"Remember, the woman in this tape is dead," Jesse said, "and she may be the victim of a crime. We are looking at evidence. Try to notice something other than her snatch."

Somebody said, "Yes sir!"

Jesse opened the mailer, took the cassette down to the other end of the table, put it in the VCR, picked up the remote, walked back to his chair, sat down and pointed the remote at the VCR.

"To serve and protect," he said and clicked PLAY.

There was a naked woman, shot from behind. She was having sex with a man who lay on his back beneath her on a bed, or sofa, or something with a blue-and-yellow stripe. As the camera watched, another man walked into the shot and mounted her.

The cops around the table cheered. Simpson was the youngest of them.

"Jesus," he said. "Front and back."

The woman turned, sandwiched between the two men, and smiled widely at the camera. It was clearly Florence Horvath. She was a lot better-looking than her license photo. Jesse smiled to himself without pleasure, *Or any other time I've seen her.* Clearly she wanted to be recognized. She kept looking back at the camera as she enjoyed her double penetration, which enjoyment she was at pains to display. Jesse didn't enjoy it much. *I can't define pornography,* he thought. But I know it when I see it, *and pro or amateur, this is it.* After about two minutes' running time, the cops began to talk. *Pornography gets boring quick,* Jesse thought.

"Between wives," Arthur Angstrom said, "I used to date a woman, wanted me to bring a friend. I told her I could never get it up with another guy involved."

"I heard you couldn't get it up anyway, Arthur," Peter Perkins said.

"Give you a list of satisfied customer, you want," Arthur said.

"Look at the weapon on that guy," Buddy Hall said.

"Jesus," Suitcase said, "if that's a penis, what am I walking around with?"

The film ended after about eight minutes with Florence apparently having an historic orgasm while the cops laughed and bantered. Jesse wondered if the banter covered any discomfort. He didn't enjoy porn very much. But he didn't mind it much unless it was gross. Jesse had always thought heterosexual anal sex verged on gross. Nothing in Florence's home movie had changed his mind about that.

"Didn't see any clues," Peter Perkins said. "Maybe we should play it more."

"Did you look at the guys?" Jesse said.

Nobody said anything.

"Okay, we'll run it again," Jesse said.

Around the table the cops groaned. Perkins had been kidding. Most of them were bored with it already.

"Look at the guys, this time," Jesse said. "Maybe we'll see one again."

Jesse rewound the tape. And rolled it. The cops watched again, looking at the men. Jesse noticed they were quieter. Less uncomfortable, maybe. Jesse looked, too. There was nothing in the film to tell him where it was shot. Just a bedroom. Or at least a place with a bed. There was a hint of decorative brass. The room looked small. *Could be a boat.*

When the tape had finished, Jesse said, "Okay, Peter, you're the evidence specialist. Take the tape and get some head shots made of the guys. May as well get one of Florence, too. It's better than her license photo."

"Guys at the lab will love this," Perkins said.

"Just make sure it comes back," Jesse said.

"You don't think they'll make a dupe?"

"Of course they will," Jesse said. "But I want the original in our case folder."

"Yessir."

Perkins started to remove the tape from the VCR.

"Leave it," Jesse said. "I'll give it to you after lunch."

"Gotta look for more clues, Jesse?"

"Chief Jesse to you, pal. Go relieve Molly on the desk. Tell her I want to see her in my office."

Perkins saluted and the cops filed out. Jesse took the tape and went in his office. In a moment Molly came in. Jesse put the tape into the office VCR.

"You know how to run this?" Jesse said.

"No."

"Okay, I'll start it and leave."

Molly nodded. Jesse punched up the tape and went out. He closed the office door behind him and leaned on the wall near it. He smiled to himself. *Porn guard.*

When Molly came out she said, "That was disgusting."

"Yes," Jesse said. "It was."

"Did the guys like it?"

Jesse shrugged.

"They pretended to. In fact, I think they probably found it a little disgusting, too."

"Did you?"

"Yes."

"You going to get head shots made?"

"Peter Perkins is going to take care of it," Jesse said.

Molly nodded. "Thanks for letting me watch it alone," she said.

Jesse shrugged.

"You're a nicer guy than most people know," Molly said.

Jesse smiled at her. "Let's not let that get around," he said.

14

When Jesse went to meet Jenn for lunch she was finishing a long Steadicam walk-and-talk the length of the town pier with the sail-dappled harbor in the background. Jesse walked down and stopped beside Marty the producer. She picked up a pair of earphones that were hanging on the back of a folding chair and handed them to Jesse. He put them on. He could hear Jenn.

"What draws them here," she was saying. "What brings them from all over the Atlantic coast to converge here . . . in Paradise . . . for Race Week."

The director who had been staring at the monitor yelled "Cut." And as Jenn looked up at him with her hands on her hips, he yelled, "Keeper." Jenn nodded as if to say *It better be,* and came up the dock toward Jesse. He applauded silently as she came. When she reached him, Jenn kissed him.

"I smell Emmy," Jesse said.

"You smell something," Jenn said and took his hand. "I'm sick of the Gull. Is there someplace else? Quick? Good?"

"We could walk up to Daisy's," Jesse said. "They bake all their own bread."

"Let's," Jenn said.

"So what does draw them?" Jesse said as they walked up Washington Street. "Top-flight police work?"

"Probably that," Jenn said. "And a full month of booze and sex."

"Anybody sail?" Jesse said.

"Not in the evening," Jenn said. "I mean, wow! Like Mardi Gras."

"For us, it's mostly fights and public urination and vandalism," Jesse said.

"Boy," Jenn said, "just like Mardi Gras."

"What's up this afternoon?" Jesse said.

"I'm off a couple hours," Jenn said. "Marty and Jake are going out and get B roll of the races."

"Without you?"

"In a helicopter."

"Without you," Jesse said.

The crowd on the streets, even at midday, was thick and boisterous. The range of dress was extreme. Horizontal-striped shirts were popular, with three-quarter-length white canvas pants. There were a lot of women in big hats and gauzy dresses. Men in blazers and white flannels. Some of the crowd looked like eighteenth-century sailors. Some of them looked like they were at Churchill Downs. Jesse wore jeans and a blue short-sleeved oxford shirt. He had his gun and badge on his belt. Two young men and two young women, all in tank tops and cutoff jeans, were walking along carrying open bottles of beer. Jesse pointed at his badge, then at the beer, then, with his thumb, at a trash container chained to the lamppost. They looked like they wanted to argue, but none of them did. They dropped the beer into the trash and moved away.

"Zero tolerance," Jesse said.

"Egad," Jenn said at Daisy's door. "Maybe we should have gone to the Gull."

The door was open and the line of people waiting was out onto the sidewalk.

"Be the same," Jesse said. "It's like this everywhere."

Several people on the sidewalk had drinks. Jesse ignored them.

"Selective enforcement?" Jenn said.

"You bet," Jesse said. "They're just waiting to have lunch. They won't do any harm. Besides, I don't want to hurt Daisy's business."

"Is there actually a Daisy?"

"I'll introduce you," Jesse said.

"But first, could you arrest somebody at a good table," Jenn said. "So we can have it."

"I'll talk to Daisy. Stay here."

Jesse slid past the crowd and in through the open door. He came back out with a strapping red-faced blond woman wearing a big white apron and holding a spatula. The woman pointed at Jenn.

"You Jenn?" she said.

"I am."

"I'm Daisy, get your ass in here," she said.

A woman in wraparound sunglasses and a large straw hat said, "We've been waiting half an hour."

"And you'll wait a lot longer," Daisy said, "you keep talking."

"But they . . ."

Daisy waved the spatula under the woman's chin.

"My restaurant," Daisy said. "I decide. Come on, Jenn."

Jenn slid sheepishly in behind Daisy, and followed her to a table by the back window where Jesse was drinking root beer. Inside, the restaurant was not crowded. The tables were well spaced and the conversation was absorbed by carpeting and sailcloth that draped the ceiling.

"Sorry I left you twisting in the wind out there," Jesse said.

Jenn sat down.

"A woman outside hates me," she said.

"Oh fuck her," Daisy said. "I can't find a table for the chief of police and his friend, what good am I?"

"Excellent point," Jenn said. "Can I have a root beer, too?"

"Sure you can, darlin', I'll send the waitress right over."

"Thank you, Daisy."

"You bet," Daisy said. "I was you I'd order one of the sandwiches, I just baked the bread this morning."

Jenn smiled. Daisy swaggered off.

"Heavens," Jenn said.

Jesse nodded.

"Daisy Dyke," he said.

"Is that her real name?"

"No, I don't know her real last name. Everybody calls her Daisy Dyke. She calls herself Daisy Dyke. She had to be talked out of calling the restaurant Daisy Dyke's."

"She is, I assume, a lesbian."

"She is."

"And she is, I assume, out."

"As far out as it is possible to be out."

"She have a partner?"

"She has a wife," Jesse said. "They got married May twentieth, right after the Massachusetts law passed."

"Mrs. Daisy Dyke?"

"Angela Carson," Jesse said. "She kept her own name."

"Is Angela a housewife?"

"Angela paints," Jesse said.

"Well?"

"No," Jesse said.

"But persistently," Jenn said.

"That would be Angela," Jesse said.

Jenn ordered an egg salad sandwich on sourdough. Jesse had a BLT on whole wheat.

"Never order that on a date," Jesse said. "Too messy."

"What the hell am I," Jenn said.

"I don't know," Jesse said, "but whatever you are, date is too small a word."

Jenn smiled at him.

"Yes," she said, "I guess it is, isn't it?"

"We'll come up with something," Jesse said.

15

With the harbormaster at the wheel, they had visited five yachts, three of them from Fort Lauderdale, anchored at the outer edge of the harbor. The harbormaster was new. His name was Hardy Watkins. He was overweight and red-faced, and, on those rare moments when he took off his long-billed cap, he was mostly bald.

"Where to next?" Watkins said.

"How about that one over there," Jesse said. "Black with a yellow stripe."

He and Suitcase Simpson stood on either side of Watkins as the squat harbor boat plugged through the low swell. Among the yachts it looked like a warthog. Jesse wore jeans and sneakers and his softball jacket over a white tee shirt. Simpson was in uniform. He carried a transparent folder with head shots from the sex video.

"Sloop there with the cutter rig," Watkins said.

"Sure," Jesse said.

He looked at Simpson.

"You know what a sloop is?" Jesse

said. "With a cutter rig?"

"Hey," Simpson said, "I grew up here. Paradise, Massachusetts, the sailing capital of the world."

"So you know what a sloop is," Jesse said. "With a cutter rig."

"No," Simpson said.

"Sloop's a single-masted boat," Watkins said.

"And a cutter?"

"Single-masted boat with the mast set further aft."

"So what's a sloop with a cutter rig."

With one hand on the wheel, Watkins pointed at the yacht ahead of them.

"That," he said.

"You don't know either," Jesse said.

"I do," Watkins said, "but you're too fucking landlocked to understand the explanation."

"Good," Jesse said.

Watkins steered the harbor boat under the stern of the yacht. The name LADY JANE was stenciled across the stern. And beneath it, MIAMI. A small landing float bobbed beside the *Lady Jane*, and Watkins brought the harbor boat softly up against it. Simpson leaned over and secured the stern of the harbor boat to a cleat. Then he climbed past the small cockpit and onto the short deck and secured the bow. Jesse climbed the short stairs to the deck of the *Lady Jane.* Simpson followed with the pictures.

A crewman in uniform met them. Jesse took his badge out of the pocket of his softball jacket and showed it.

"I'm Jesse Stone, Paradise Police. This is Officer Simpson."

"I'm Nils Borgman," the crewman said with a small accent. "First mate."

Jesse glanced around the yacht.

"Sloop with a cutter rig," he said.

"Yes sir," Borgman said. "It is."

Simpson looked carefully out to sea.

"I'll need to talk to everyone on board," Jesse said. "Who do I see about that."

"What is this about, sir?" Borgman said.

"Investigating the death of a young woman, we're trying to find anyone who recognizes her."

"Do you need a warrant or something for that?" Borgman said.

"No," Jesse said.

"I'll speak to the captain, sir. I'm sure he'll consult with Mr. Darnell."

"Mr. Darnell is the owner of this cutter-rigged sloop?" Jesse said.

"Yes sir. Please wait here."

Jesse and Simpson waited, squinting in the brightness of the sun and its seaborne reflection. Below them the harbor boat swayed gently against the boarding float. Watkins was sitting behind the tiller reading a book, the long bill of his cap pulled low to keep the sun from his eyes. A dozen other yachts rode anchor in sight, and back in the harbor, the clutter of smaller boats seeming closer together from the deck of the *Lady Jane* than they actually were.

The deck was dark polished wood. Probably teak, Jesse thought, or some other wood that could resist the salt water. Polished brass was nearly everywhere. Under a canopy in the cockpit lunch was being eaten and drunk, by a group of three men and three women, seated on built-in couches on either side of a built-in table. A man in a hat with lots of gold braid came from forward into the dining area and spoke softly to one of the men at lunch. The man listened and nodded and turned to look at Jesse and Simpson. Then he got up and walked back to them.

"Harrison Darnell," he said. "What's all this?"

"We're investigating the death of a young woman," Jesse said, "and we need to show some pictures to everyone on board, see if they recognize anyone."

"I'll discuss this with my attorney, if you don't mind," Darnell said.

"I don't mind," Jesse said. "Of course, I guess we'll need to round up everybody on board and bring them into the station for questioning."

"You can't do that."

"Of course I can, Mr. Darnell. But by all means call your attorney first."

Mr. Darnell was wearing blue flip-flops, pale khaki shorts and a red short-sleeved shirt decorated with a pattern of blue flowers. The shirt was open. He wore some sort of braided leather around his neck. His hairless chest was tanned, as was the rest of him. His blond hair was shoulder length, kept off his face by sunglasses worn, as if pushed up casually, on his head. His face was old enough looking so that Jesse suspected artifice in the hair color. You didn't often see a man with absolutely no hair on his chest, Jesse thought. Jesse wondered if Darnell shaved it. Maybe it was gray.

"Oh for crissake," Darnell said.

He turned back into the lunch area.

"People," he said. "I'm sorry. The local gendarmes wish to show you some pictures. They've promised it won't take long."

One blond woman with a long oval face

squealed as she turned and looked at them.

"Ohmigod," she said. "The fuzz."

She was wearing a bikini bathing suit and huge sunglasses. She had a nearly empty glass of champagne in her hand. Because she was sitting on a blue-and-yellow-striped couch, Jesse couldn't see well enough to be sure, but he was confident that the bikini bottom was a thong.

"Show them the pictures," Jesse said.

Suit stepped to the table and showed them to the blonde. Jesse watched her face. It was why he had Simpson show the pictures, so he could stand and look for a reaction. She barely glanced at the photographs.

"Nobody I know," she said and looked back at Jesse.

"How come he's wearing a uniform and you're not?" she said, and emptied her champagne glass and held it out toward the crew member in charge of pouring. He refilled it.

"I'm the chief," Jesse said. "I get to wear what I want."

Simpson showed the picture to the man beside the blonde. The blonde drank some champagne.

"And you chose that?" she said.

Jesse was studying the face of the man

79

looking at the pictures.

"They do call it *plain* clothes," Jesse said.

She drank again and shifted a little so he could see the line of her thigh better. Jesse kept his eyes on her companions, as, one at a time, they looked at the pictures.

"Are you carrying your gun?" the blonde said.

"In case of pirates," Jesse said.

The blonde took a cigarette from a silver cigarette case. The man next to her snapped a lighter. She inhaled deeply and took a drink of champagne and let the smoke out through her nose while she swallowed. Simpson showed the pictures to the final person at the table. No one recognized them and no one had shown any reaction to them.

"There, now can you have a nice drink?" the blonde said.

"Show it to the crew," Jesse said to Simpson.

"Well, isn't he a good big boy," the blonde said, "doing everything the chief says."

Jesse was studying each crew member as the pictures were shown. No recognition, no reaction.

"Why do you keep staring at everybody," the blonde said.

"Clues," Jesse said, "I'm looking for clues."

"Oh pooh," the blonde said. "Why don't you join us for a nice cocktail?"

"What could be better?" Jesse said. "Except I'm afraid that Suit here would rat me out to the Board of Selectmen."

"Why do you call him Suit?" the blonde said.

Amazing, Jesse thought, *no matter what she says, she manages to make it sound like a challenge.* Jesse nodded at Suit.

"My name's Simpson, ma'am, and there used to be a ballplayer named Suitcase Simpson, so the guys started calling me that, and it sort of got shortened to Suit."

She laughed and finished her glass of champagne and held it out toward the pourer.

"What a boring answer," she said.

"Begging your pardon, ma'am," Simpson said. "The question wasn't all that interesting, either."

The blonde had a full glass again. She drank, and took in a big inhale and held it for a while before she let it out slowly, blowing the smoke out in a thin stream toward Jesse and Simpson. She shook her head.

"Local yokels," she said and turned away back toward her lunch mates.

Darnell had been standing throughout

the picture showing. Now he stepped forward. He was taller than Jesse and exaggerated the difference in height by bending forward to speak.

"If there's nothing else," he said.

"Can't guarantee that," Jesse said. "But there's nothing else right now."

He took a card case from his jacket pocket, took out a number of cards and tossed them on the lunch table.

"If anyone has anything, remembers anything, sees any of these people, whatever, please call me."

The blonde ostentatiously reached out, picked up one of the cards, looked at it for a moment and then tucked it into the top of her bikini bottom.

"Maybe I'll call you, Jesse," she said.

"Or e-mail me," Jesse said. "Localyokel.com."

Hanging from the corner of the dining area, there was an ornamental brass monkey sitting on an ornamental brass trapeze bar, with a long brass ornamental tail. Jesse stopped to look at it.

"Not anatomically correct," Jesse said. "Must have been very cold somewhere."

He chucked the monkey under its chin, smiled at the lunch crowd and went down the ladder behind Simpson.

16

Jesse was in his office watching the Florence Horvath sex video when Jenn knocked and entered without waiting.

"Jesse, I . . ."

She stared at the screen.

"Jesse, you pervert," she said.

"Evidence," Jesse said. "Care to watch?"

Jenn stood for a minute looking at the threesome on the screen.

"Oh, ick!" she said.

Jesse clicked the remote. The image froze. He clicked again. The screen went dark. Jenn wrinkled her nose.

"I'm looking for something," Jesse said.

"I hope so," Jenn said. "The image of you sitting alone in your office watching a gang bang is not a pretty one."

"I think a gang bang requires more people," Jesse said. "This is more a ménage à trois, I believe."

"It's a ménage à yuck," Jenn said. "What are you looking for?"

"Something I saw on a yacht yesterday afternoon," Jesse said. "A brass monkey with a long brass tail, and I have some sort of subliminal memory that I saw something like it, or part of it, or something brass, on this tape."

"A brass monkey tail," Jenn said.

"Yeah," Jesse said. "And the couch on the boat where they were eating lunch was the same color as the bed she's having her liaison on."

"Blue-and-yellow stripe," Jenn said.

"Wow, you journalists are observant."

"I think the correct phrase is still *weather weenie*," Jenn said. "At least until after they air my Race Week special."

"Okay, ween," Jesse said. "You're still observant, want to help me watch?"

"Okay," Jenn said, "but you better not enjoy it."

Jesse clicked the remote again. The tape proceeded. Jesse and Jenn watched silently. As Florence shifted slightly in her delight, the camera moved right to stay on her, and something gleamed fractionally in the right corner of the screen.

"There," Jenn said.

Jesse froze the frame, but it was past the flash. He rewound, and went forward and froze the frame again, and this time he got it. Curling into the picture was a brass monkey tail.

"Every person on that boat said they didn't recognize anyone in the pictures," Jesse said.

"It doesn't actually prove that it's the same boat."

"No, but it's a pretty good coincidence," Jesse said. "And coincidence just isn't useful in cop work."

"What are you going to do?"

"Get some stills made," Jesse said.

"Then what?" Jenn said. "Confront them with it?"

"First I think I'll check more on the boat. Some of those yachts are rented. These people may not have been aboard when Florence was. I need to be sure it has been around these parts long enough. She was in the water awhile."

Jenn nodded.

"Why do you think she made that tape?" Jenn said.

"I don't know," Jesse said. "Could have been money."

"That seems more like a home movie," Jenn said. "Video camera with a light bar."

"You would know amateur from professional?" Jesse said.

Jenn shrugged.

"I've seen a few porn films," she said.

"And?"

"And nothing," Jenn said. "I didn't enjoy them."

"But your date thought you would?" Jesse said.

Jenn shook her head and didn't say anything. Jesse reeled himself back in.

"I have known women," he said, "who were interested in seeing themselves having sex on film."

"With two men at the same time?" Jenn said.

Jesse shrugged.

"Do you have any idea," Jenn said, "how . . . how a thing like that would make a woman feel?"

"The men, too," Jesse said.

Jenn looked startled.

"Yes," she said. "I suppose that's right. It doesn't glamorize them, either."

Jesse nodded.

"Most women I know don't like that," Jenn said.

"No," Jesse said.

"But men do," Jenn said.

"More than women, probably," Jesse said. "Most men will look. Most men wouldn't want to spend too much time looking. And almost all men know that it gets old really quick."

"Why would you want to look at something that turns you into a thing?" Jenn said.

Jesse was quiet. They were veering into Dix territory again.

"You're a man," Jenn said. "Why do you think men are like that?"

This was about more than pornography, and in some visceral way Jesse realized that it was about him. He took in some air.

"This could turn quickly into psychobabble," Jesse said. "But you've had enough shrink time to know what some of the reasons might be."

"Objectification is control," Jenn said.

Jesse nodded.

"Of what?" Jenn said.

Jesse shook his head and shrugged.

"Of the object," he said.

"Are you still talking to Dix?" Jenn said.

"Some."

"Well, you better keep it up," Jenn said. " 'Cause you're getting crazier."

17

Jesse sat in his car on the tip of Paradise Neck, at Lighthouse Point. The car windows were down. The sea air was coming in gently, and he was looking at the *Lady Jane* with a pair of good binoculars. The sailboat races were under way east of Stiles Island, and several of the yachts anchored at the harbor mouth had moved out to watch. *Lady Jane* stayed at anchor. They hadn't come for the races. They'd come for the cocktails. Jesse could count six people and three crew from where he sat, though he couldn't see well enough to pick out Darnell or the mouthy blonde. He couldn't see the brass monkey, either.

Molly called him on his cell phone.

"Why don't you ever take your official chief car?" Molly said. "I keep trying to raise you on the radio."

"I like mine better," Jesse said.

"Christ," Molly said. "You don't drive the car, you hardly ever wear your uniform, you don't use the department issue gun. What's wrong with you anyway?"

"More than we have time to examine," Jesse said. "What's up?"

"Two things," Molly said. "One, the *Lady Jane* is in fact out of Miami, owned by Harrison Darnell."

"Un-huh."

"And, two, Detective Kelly Cruz of Fort Lauderdale PD wants you to call her on her cell phone. If you'd been in the company car I could have patched her through to the radio."

"How many kids you got, Molly?" Jesse said.

"Four, you know that."

"And am I one of them?" Jesse said.

"Oh go fuck yourself . . . sir."

"Give me Cruz's cell phone number," Jesse said.

Molly told him, Jesse wrote it down and smiled as he broke the connection. He dialed Kelly Cruz.

"Couple things," Jesse said. "You guys got that tape dated yet?"

"No," Kelly Cruz said. "Don't have the budget for it."

"Okay, you owed me," Jesse said. "You got a date?"

"Lab found a date and time stamp," she said. "March seventh, this year, at three-oh-nine in the afternoon."

"And I think I know where," Jesse said.

"Really?"

"Cockpit of a yacht named *Lady Jane* out of Miami," Jesse said.

"Cockpit's appropriate," Kelly said. "You know who owns the boat?"

"Harrison Darnell," Jesse said.

"Address?"

"I'll have Molly Crane call you as soon as we stop talking," Jesse said. "She's got it."

"Okay. You know where the yacht is now?"

"Here," Jesse said.

"Mr. Darnell aboard?"

"Yes."

"I'll check on him," Kelly Cruz said. "I got people I can call in Miami."

"Appreciate it," Jesse said. "Got anything else?"

"Talked to the parents," she said.

"Mr. and Mrs. Plum?"

"Yes. They live in Miami."

"Close at hand," Jesse said.

"Sure, 'bout twenty miles from me. They didn't know even where she was living, they said. They had no communication with her, and hadn't for a couple years."

"Any, ah, precipitating incident?" Jesse said.

"Wow," Kelly Cruz said. "Precipitating incident. Not really, they just, they said, were at the end of their tether. Her grandfather, guy that founded Plum and Partridge, left her a ton of money in trust until she turned twenty-five. When she got it, they told me, she was pretty smart with the money."

"So she got richer," Jesse said.

"Yeah. She lived high up on the hog," Kelly Cruz said, "off the invested principal."

"That an issue?"

"Yeah. She drank too much, did too much dope, fucked whoever stopped by. They think she's some kind of bad seed. But whenever she'd get drunk or strung out or pregnant, or divorced, she'd come home until she straightened out. Then she'd fight with her parents and her two younger sisters and disappear again."

"How old are the sisters?"

"Twenty," Kelly Cruz said. "They're twins."

"Our ME says she was mid-thirties."

"Thirty-four," she said.

"Fourteen years," Jesse said.

"I know. They didn't comment," Kelly Cruz said. "But they felt she was a bad influence on her sisters and last time she left they told her not to come back."

"Talk to the sisters?"

"Nope. They're spending the summer in Europe."

"Plum and Partridge doing okay?"

"Very well," Kelly Cruz said. "You should see where they live."

"They got any theories on Florence's death?" Jesse said.

"No," Kelly Cruz said. "But I think they feel she deserved it."

"Home is where the heart is," Jesse said.

"You got kids?" she said.

"No."

"I got two," she said. "No matter what they did or what they turned into, they could never deserve it."

"What are the twins' names?" Jesse said.

"You'll love this," Kelly Cruz said, "wait a minute, I got it in my notes. . . . Corliss and Claudia. Isn't that sweet? Corliss and Claudia Plum."

"When are they coming back from Europe?"

"Don't know. Probably in time for senior year at school."

"What school?"

"Emory," Kelly Cruz said.

"When you talk with Molly about Darnell's address, could you leave her the

Plums' address, and phone?"

"Sure," she said. "You coming down?"

"Maybe if the case runs into winter," Jesse said.

"Lemme know," Kelly Cruz said. "You'll be on expenses and I can get us into Joe's Stone Crab."

"Sure," Jesse said. "You tell the parents about the sex tape?"

"No."

"You didn't have the heart."

"That's right."

"Show them head shots from the tape?" Jesse said. "The two guys?"

"Yes. They didn't recognize either one."

"Thanks, Kelly," Jesse said. "I know you got other cases, but anything comes across your desk . . ."

"I'm a curious girl," Kelly Cruz said. "And sometimes it's slow around here. I get time I'll look up Harrison Darnell, and I'll sniff around when I can."

They hung up. Jesse sat looking at the *Lady Jane* without the binoculars.

"I wouldn't have told them about the video, either," he said aloud to no one.

18

Molly stuck her head in the door to Jesse's office.

"Lady to see you, Jess."

Jesse nodded. Molly went away and came back in a moment with the mouthy blonde from the *Lady Jane.* She was wearing sunglasses, a backless yellow halter sundress with large blue flowers, and white slingback shoes with three-inch heels. The dress came to about the middle of her thighs.

"The local yokel," she said.

"Chief Yokel," Jesse said.

"You really are the chief of police," she said.

"I am," Jesse said.

She came in and sat opposite him. She crossed her legs. The skirt of the sundress slid further back on her tan thighs. She placed her small yellow straw purse in her lap and opened it.

"Mind if I smoke?" she said.

"I do," Jesse said.

"You mind?"

"Yes."

She had the silver cigarette case halfway out of her purse.

"You do mind?" she said.

"I do," Jesse said.

"Jesus Christ!" she said.

She put the case back in her purse.

"I knew you were so prissy," the blonde said, "I wouldn't have come to help you."

Jesse was quiet.

The blonde said, "You got any coffee at least?"

"Sure," Jesse said.

He got her some.

"Cream and sugar?"

She shook her head. He handed her the cup. She took a sip.

"Well," she said. "It's strong."

Jesse nodded. The blonde sipped coffee, and looked around the room.

"Are you carrying your gun, Chief Yokel?"

"Always armed and ready," Jesse said.

The blonde seemed somehow to wiggle motionlessly.

"Really?" she said.

Jesse smiled. The blonde smiled back. Her teeth were very white. Dental intervention, Jesse assumed. *Bonding or whitening or glazing or whatever the hell.*

"My name's Blondie Martin," she said.

"Jesse Stone."

"I know," Blondie said, "the police chief. You told us on the boat."

Jesse nodded.

"Have you always been the chief of police?" Blondie said.

"No."

"So how long have you been Chief Local Yokel?"

"About seven years," Jesse said.

"What before?"

"I was a cop in Los Angeles," Jesse said.

"Oh my," Blondie said, "a not-so-local yokel."

Jesse didn't say anything. Blondie crossed her legs the other way. She drank some more coffee, holding the white mug in both hands.

"You married?" she said.

"Sort of," he said.

"How can you be sort of married?"

"My ex-wife and I are giving it another try," Jesse said.

"Some people just won't let go," she said.

Jesse nodded. She drank the rest of her coffee and stood and poured herself another cup from the Mister Coffee on top of the file cabinet. Standing, she sipped her coffee, and looked sideways at Jesse and smiled.

"Remember I said I'd come to help you?" she said.

"Yes."

"Are you wondering what help I'm bringing?"

"Yes."

"Well, you are certainly calm about it."

"I try," Jesse said.

"What was that sports jacket you were wearing on the boat?"

"Paradise Twi-league," Jesse said. "Softball."

"What's your position?"

"Shortstop."

"Are you good?"

"Yes."

"Very good?"

"Yes."

"You look like you'd be very good," Blondie said. "If you're so good, why aren't you playing someplace instead of being Chief Yokel?"

"Hurt my shoulder," Jesse said. "Can't throw much anymore."

"But you're still playing."

"I can throw enough for the Paradise Twi-league," Jesse said. "Not for the Show."

"Show?"

"Big leagues," Jesse said.

"Were you good enough for the, ah,

Show, before you got hurt?"

"Yes."

"Bummer," Blondie said.

Jesse waited. She drank more coffee. She couldn't smoke. He wasn't serving cocktails. Any stimulant in a pinch.

"At least two people on the *Lady Jane* were lying to you the other day," Blondie said.

"Happens a lot," Jesse said.

"Harrison knew those two guys in the pictures you showed us."

Jesse waited.

"They crewed for him last year. I was on the boat with him a few times last year. I recognized them both."

"Anyone else that should have recognized them?" Jesse said.

"No, just Harrison and me."

"Why didn't you tell me on the boat?"

"Didn't want Harrison getting mad. I'm a long way from home and he's my ride back."

"Where's home?"

"Palm Beach. Harrison picked me up there and we came on up for Race Week."

"You with him?" Jesse said.

"Sort of, I guess," Blondie said. "Got to be with somebody."

19

Jesse was at his desk, checking overtime slips and drinking coffee, when Molly stuck her head in.

"Wait'll you get a load of this," she said.

Jesse looked up.

"More sex tapes?"

"Live action," Molly said. "The sisters Plum."

"Florence Horvath's sisters?"

"In the, ah, flesh," Molly said.

Jesse put the neat pile of overtime slips aside.

"Bring them in," he said.

Corliss and Claudia Plum were very blond, very slim, very tanned and very slightly dressed. They wore very dark eye makeup, very light lipstick. One of them had on a sleeveless aqua-and-coral patterned summer dress with a short skirt, and showed very deep cleavage. The other had on a robin's-egg-blue-and-pink dress of the same length, and showed lots of cleavage. Both wore slip-on shoes with very high heels. One pair was aqua, the other was blue. Neither wore stockings. It was also clear that neither was wearing a bra. Jesse stood when they came in.

Aqua and coral said, "I'm Corliss."

Blue and pink said, "I'm Claudia."

"Jesse Stone."

Both girls shook his hand and then sat without much regard to the minimal length of their dresses.

Well, Jesse thought, *at least they're wearing underpants.*

"I'm very sorry about your sister," Jesse said.

"That's why we're here," Claudia said.

"We want to know the truth," Corliss said.

"We found your sister floating in the harbor," Jesse said.

"So who killed her," Corliss said.

"We don't know that anyone did."

"You don't know? How come you don't know. You think she just jumped in the ocean?"

"We don't know exactly how she got in the ocean," Jesse said.

"Well, she sure didn't jump in," Claudia said.

"Do you have a theory?" Jesse said.

"What about DNA?"

"We know her identity," Jesse said. "Why

do you think someone killed her?"

"She wouldn't just fall in," Corliss said.

"Did she drink?" Jesse said.

"Course," Corliss said. "But she could handle it, she wouldn't get drunk and fall in the ocean."

Jesse nodded.

"I thought you were in Europe," Jesse said.

The twins looked at each other.

"That's what we told the parents," Claudia said.

They both giggled.

"Partying," Corliss said.

"Where?"

"In New York."

"Manhattan?" Jesse asked.

"No, no, Sag Harbor."

"All summer?"

Both girls giggled.

"Staying with friends?"

"Ohhh yes," Corliss said.

"Could I have a name?" Jesse said.

"Name?"

"Of the friend you stayed with."

"Why?"

"Better to know than not know," Jesse said.

"You think we did something bad?" Claudia said.

"Ohhh yeah," Jesse said, and smiled.

The twins giggled again.

"Well, we didn't do anything bad to Flo," Claudia said.

"Of course not," Jesse said. "Where were you staying on Long Island?"

"Well," Corliss looked at her sister.

"We were at a guy's house in Sag Harbor."

"Name?"

"Ah, the guy that owned the house was, ah, Carlo."

Jesse nodded and waited. Corliss looked at her sister again.

"What was Carlo's last name?" she said. "You remember?"

Claudia frowned cutely.

"Funny name," she said, "like it was part of his first name."

Corliss frowned cutely. Jesse waited.

"Like Coca-Cola," Corliss said.

"Carlo Coca," Claudia said.

"C-O-C-A?" Jesse said.

"I guess," Claudia said.

Both twins looked pleased. Jesse wrote down the name.

"Got an address?" Jesse said.

"Oh," Claudia said, "I don't know."

She looked at Corliss.

"On the beach," Corliss said.

"Phone?"

They both shrugged. Jesse nodded.

"Well, we'll find him," Jesse said.

"He may not remember us," Corliss said.

Jesse smiled at them.

"Hard not to," he said.

"You can't tell our parents," Claudia said.

"They'd have a shit fit," Corliss said.

"I have no reason to tell your parents," Jesse said.

"They think we're still their little baby virgins," Claudia said.

"How did you hear of Florence's death?" Jesse said.

"One of our friends called," Corliss said.

"The friend knew where you were?"

"Not really, she called on our cell phone."

"What's her name?"

"Kimmy," Corliss said.

"Kimmy Young," Claudia said. "Why?"

"I'm a cop," Jesse said. "I like to know stuff."

"We were thinking maybe we should hire some kind of private detective," Corliss said.

Jesse nodded.

"You know?" Corliss said.

Jesse nodded again.

"I mean this is like a small town,"

Claudia said. "You know?"

"I do," Jesse said.

"So you won't be like, insulted?" Corliss said.

"No."

"But we don't know how to go about it," Claudia said.

Jesse nodded.

"Talk with Rita Fiore," Jesse said.

He wrote the name and phone number on a piece of yellow paper and handed it to Claudia.

"Criminal lawyer at a big Boston firm," Jesse said. "Use my name. I'm sure she can put you in touch with someone."

"We, ah, forgot your name," Corliss said.

Jesse took a card from the middle drawer of his desk and handed it to Corliss.

"She'll be, ah, you know, she won't talk about us to anyone," Corliss said.

"Soul of discretion," Jesse said.

They nodded.

"Are you planning to stay awhile?"

"Until our sister's killer is brought to justice," Corliss said.

"Before you leave here this morning, give Molly your address."

"Is that the policewoman out front?"

Jesse smiled. Molly would bite them if they called her that.

"At the desk," he said.

"Okay. We got a nice suite at the Four Seasons. With a view."

"In Boston," Jesse said.

"Un-huh," Corliss said.

"Did anything bad happen to Flo before she died?" Claudia said.

"Hard to say."

"I mean did anybody hurt her?"

"Can't tell," Jesse said. "You think someone would?"

The twins looked at each other.

"Not really," Corliss said. "But she ran with a weird crowd sometimes."

"Names?" Jesse said.

Both twins shook their heads.

"Oh, we don't know that," Claudia said.

"We don't know any of them really," Corliss said.

Jesse took the sex video head shots from a drawer and put them out on the desk where the Plum twins could see them.

"Know either of these gentlemen?" Jesse said.

They did. Jesse could tell by the way their shoulders froze when they looked. They both shook their heads at the same time.

"No," Claudia said.

"No, we don't," Corliss said.

Jesse took out three other pictures.

"One of these Florence?" Jesse said.

They looked.

"Course," Corliss said.

"That one," Claudia said.

"You didn't even know which one she was?"

"I did," Jesse said. "I wanted to be sure you did."

They both stared at him silently for a moment.

Then Claudia said, "Jesus Christ."

Corliss said, "Don't you trust anybody?"

"Trust," Jesse said, "but verify."

"What's that mean?"

"It's a reference to Ronald Reagan," Jesse said.

"That president?"

"Him," Jesse said.

"Well, I think it's mean not to trust us," Claudia said.

"You're right," Jesse said. "I'll never do it again."

20

After the twins were gone, Molly stuck her head in the office door.

"Steve Friedman called in," she said. "Got a couple of kids shoplifting in Waldo's Variety Store."

"What did they take?"

"Skin magazines."

"Tell Steve to confiscate the magazines, let the kids sit in the cruiser for ten minutes to scare them, then kick 'em loose. No lectures."

Molly grinned.

"That'll be hard for Steve," she said.

"I know. Tell him I said so."

"No parent notification?" Molly said.

"No."

Molly was still grinning.

"How were the twins?" Molly said.

"Vague," Jesse said.

"You survive with your virtue intact?"

"So much sex," Jesse said, "so little brain."

"You learn anything useful?" Molly said.

"Mostly I learned that they know more

than they are saying, and that they conceal that fact badly."

"What do you think they know?"

"They know the two guys in the sex video," Jesse said.

"They say so?"

"No."

"What did they want?"

"I don't think they quite know," Jesse said. "They asked me to recommend a private eye."

"To help us on the case?"

"Un-huh."

Molly rolled her eyes.

"There are some good ones," Jesse said. "I sent the little darlings to Rita Fiore, told them she could recommend."

"Can she?"

"Probably. I know she uses some guy in Boston that's supposed to be good."

"You think they were serious?"

"I don't think they've been serious in their whole vapid life, either one of them."

"And you sent them to Rita," Molly said, "so you could call her in a while and asked if they showed up."

Jesse smiled and pointed a finger at Molly.

"You're mastering my technique," Jesse said. "When I leave, you can be chief."

"Fat chance," Molly said. "I better get on the horn to Steve. He's probably already started his lecture."

"Cruel and unusual punishment," Jesse said.

"Wading through the skin magazines would be cruel enough," Molly said.

"Not if you're an adolescent boy," Jesse said.

"You would know," Molly said and left the office.

Jesse stood and walked to the door.

"Be sure Steve brings in the confiscated magazines," he said.

21

Jesse was on the small balcony off the living room, drinking club soda, with his shirt off, when Jenn came home. It was hot, but the air off the harbor was cool and as the sun went down it got cooler. When they had been married and worked in Los Angeles, Jesse and Jenn had lived in one of those old bungalows in Hollywood, with an over-hanging roof and a big front porch. Jesse used to like to sit out on the front steps of the porch in his undershirt and drink beer and feel the air.

She kissed him gently when she came in.

"I'll join you," she said. "Thank God it's evening."

She went to the kitchen and got some white wine and brought it with her to the balcony and sat in the other chair.

It was late enough to be dark. Jenn sipped her wine. Many of the boats in the harbor showed lights, particularly the big yachts farther out. The black water moved quietly below them. In daylight there was usually some trash floating on it. In the darkness it was unmarred. Barely visible, its presence announced mostly by its dark movement.

"Domestic," Jenn said after a time.

"That's us," Jesse said.

"I mean it," Jenn said, "as a good thing."

"I know," Jesse said.

"Just sitting together," Jenn said. "At the end of the day."

"Maybe I should buy a couple of rocking chairs," Jesse said.

"And a shawl," Jenn said.

Jesse looked at his glass.

"Nothing like a bracing club soda," he said, "at moments like this."

"You still miss it," Jenn said.

"Every day."

"Is it a physical craving?"

"No, never quite has been a craving," Jesse said. "It's just, I like it and I miss it."

Jenn smiled.

"Like me," she said.

"No," Jesse said. "You're a craving."

They were quiet for a time. There was a dim sound of music from among the moored boats in near shore. Across the harbor, they could see the running lights of a powerboat moving silently along the inner shoreline of the Neck.

"Glad I'm ahead of Johnny Walker,"

Jenn said after a time.

Jenn drank the rest of her wine and went to pour a second glass. Jesse drank some soda, and put his feet on the balcony railing. He crossed his ankles. The running lights of the powerboat turned silently and began to trace the causeway at the south end of the harbor. Jenn came back.

"You know," Jesse said. "Craving is pretty much all about the craver and nothing about the cravee."

"No shit," Jenn said.

Jenn had kicked off her shoes. She put her feet up on the balcony next to his. It made her skirt slide up her thighs. Jesse felt the surge of desire. *What was that about?* He'd seen her naked a thousand times. He'd had sex with her a thousand times. Why did he feel this way because her skirt slid up her thighs? He'd always assumed such feelings were the result of normal masculine humanity.

"I'm leering at your thighs," Jesse said.

"Good."

"You want to be desired, you dress sexy, you look sexy, you want to be seen as sexy. We both know that."

"And we both know you are making something out of nothing, Looney Tunes," Jenn said. "You're supposed to get riled up looking at my thighs, for crissake. You're supposed to leer."

"Looney Tunes," Jesse said.

"It's like we don't have problems anymore," Jenn said. "And you're trying to invent some."

Jesse wished he had a drink. He shrugged.

"Anyway," Jesse said. "It was a loving leer."

22

Molly came into Jesse's office and stood in front of his desk.

"I called the registrar at Emory," she said. "The Plum sisters haven't been students there since first semester last year."

"I assume they didn't graduate."

"No, they left school after first semester of their junior year."

"Did they say why?"

"They didn't say anything. They just ceased to be there." Molly smiled.

"They didn't get the boot or anything?"

"No. Just stopped going."

"Take all their belongings?" Jesse said.

"I don't know. I can check back."

"Please," Jesse said.

Molly went out. Jesse picked up his phone and called Kelly Cruz in Fort Lauderdale.

"Know anything new about the Plum sisters?" Jesse said.

"Models of decorous southern behavior," Kelly Cruz said.

"Decorous?"

"I'm taking a night course," Kelly Cruz

said, "at the community college. So far that's what I've learned."

"Who says they're, ah, decorous?" Jesse said.

"Mom and Dad."

"You check with anyone else?"

"Not yet," Kelly Cruz said. "I told you, this isn't the big one on my caseload, you know? This is yours."

"And here's what I know," Jesse said. "The Plum girls haven't been in Europe looking at art. They've been in Sag Harbor, Long Island, partying. And they dropped out of Emory last fall."

"But did they do it decorously?" Kelly Cruz said.

"I think we need to know more."

"Wonder what else the parents don't know?" Kelly Cruz said.

"Or do know and aren't saying. What do you know about the three yachts registered in Fort Lauderdale?"

"Thomas Ralston, Allan Pinkton, Harold Berger," Kelly Cruz said.

"Wow," Jesse said.

"Thank you," Kelly Cruz said. "Berger is up there with his wife and three children. Pinkton has his grown daughters and their husbands aboard, along with their combined four children, and his wife."

"How about Ralston."

"Owns the *Sea Cloud*," Kelly Cruz said. "He's single, up there with some guests."

"Find anything on Harrison Darnell?"

"Family money," she said. "Been rich for a couple generations. Real estate development. Never married. Playboy reputation. No record."

"Never married," Jesse said.

"Everyone concurs that he's straight, and actively so."

"Hence the playboy rep," Jesse said.

"Hence," Kelly Cruz said.

"How about Darnell? Any connection between him and Ralston?"

"They're about the same age," Kelly Cruz said. "Single playboys who live in South Florida and own yachts which they sailed up to Paradise for Race Week. They could easily know each other."

"Or not," Jesse said.

"Or not," Kelly Cruz said. "I'll look into it."

"How about the ex-husbands?"

"Aside from Horvath? Can't find one of them. He's not in the area, wherever he is. The other one is convinced she was a nymphomaniac."

"I don't think we use that term anymore, do we?" Jesse said.

"This guy does, with an accent. He's an Argentine polo player."

"When were they married?"

"Nineteen ninety-four, ninety-five," Kelly Cruz said.

"Divorced?"

"Nineteen ninety-five," Kelly Cruz said. "Sex life was hurting his game."

"Tired all the time?"

"That's what he says."

"He get a nice settlement?" Jesse asked.

"Yes."

"You know where he's been the last couple of months?"

"Playing polo. Every day. In Miami. I checked the papers. He was there."

"There's polo writeups in the papers down there?"

"You know what papers to look in," Kelly Cruz said.

"Okay. So he's not a prime suspect."

"Too bad, I was hoping I'd need to interview him more."

"Didn't you say you had kids?"

"I did, but no husband."

"And rich polo players make notoriously good fathers," Jesse said.

"Notoriously," Kelly Cruz said.

"What you need to do," Jesse said, "is see if there's a connection between Ralston and Darnell. And I think you need to pressure the parents. There's too much going on that we don't understand."

"No more Miss Nice Girl?" Kelly Cruz said.

"Exactly."

"Okay, I need to do that," Kelly Cruz said. "What do you need?"

"I need to get a look at their boats," Jesse said.

23

"You go on the boat without a warrant," Molly said, "nothing you find can be used as evidence."

"I don't have enough for a warrant."

"Not even Judge Gaffney?" Molly said.

Jesse shook his head.

"Marty Reagan says the new DA is very careful."

"So he won't even ask," Molly said.

"Right."

"So what's the point of going aboard?"

"Better to know than not know."

"Even if you can't use it."

"Can't use it in court," Jesse said. "But maybe it'll point me toward something I can use."

"Be good to know if they're viable suspects," Molly said.

"It would," Jesse said.

"Be good to know if they weren't viable suspects," Molly said.

"Also true," Jesse said.

"So you could start looking someplace else."

"Um-hm."

"Of course, it's illegal," Molly said.

"Nobody's perfect," Jesse said.

Molly nodded slowly.

"You cut some corners, Jesse."

"Sometimes you have to, if you're going to do the job right."

"So you do something wrong to do something right?"

"Sometimes," Jesse said.

"I'm not sure Sister Mary Agnes would agree," Molly said.

"Sister Mary Agnes a cop?" Jesse said.

Molly smiled.

"She taught Philosophy of Christian Ethics at Our Lady of the Annunciation Academy."

"Certainties are harder to come by," Jesse said, "in police work."

"But there's a danger, isn't there," Molly said, "that you start cutting corners and you end up doing bad, not good?"

"Yes, there is," Jesse said.

"Do you worry about that?"

"Yes," Jesse said, "I do."

"But you'll do it anyway."

"Sometimes," Jesse said. "I trust myself to keep it clean."

"Pride goeth before a fall is what Sister Mary Agnes would say."

"Sometimes," Jesse said, "it goeth before an indictment."

Molly smiled at him.

"I guess, if I'm going to have somebody bending the law on me," she said, "I'd just as soon it be you."

"Better than Mary Agnes?"

"Sister dealt mostly in theory," Molly said.

"Like when they do marriage counseling," Jesse said.

"Do I hear anti-Catholicism?"

"No," Jesse said, "anti-theory-ism."

Molly smiled again. "You better hide your tracks," she said, "in case you do get them in court. You don't one of those fruit from the poisoned tree things."

"You're still taking those law courses," Jesse said. "Aren't you."

"One a semester," Molly said.

"Different than Philosophy of Christian Ethics?"

"Just as theoretical," Molly said.

"But more commonly applied," Jesse said.

"By people like us," Molly said.

"You'll be DA someday."

"I was thinking more about president," Molly said. "How are you planning to search the boat without getting caught."

"Everybody," Jesse said, "goes to the Stiles Island Clambake."

"Second Saturday in Race Week," Molly said.

"Which is tomorrow," Jesse said.

"Midpoint of Race Week," Molly said.

"Was Race Week ever just a week?"

"I think so," Molly said, "but sometime back when my mother was in high school it started expanding at both ends. The small boats the first two weeks, the big yacht races the second two. With the clambake in the middle."

"But they still call it Race Week," Jesse said.

"Race Month just doesn't sound right," Molly said.

"But it is the social occasion. Everybody goes."

"Except me, this year," Molly said. "I'm right here three to eleven. Applying legal theory."

"And I'll be out in the harbor," Jesse said, "committing piracy."

"Shiver me timbers," Molly said.

24

The caterer's clambake crew started Friday afternoon, digging a hole two feet deep and fifteen feet across. They lined it with rocks, built a bonfire on top of the rocks and let it burn, feeding it through the night with hardwood. In the morning, when the fire had burned down, they spread seaweed over the rocks and then began layering in clams, lobsters, corn on the cob, potatoes and thick Portuguese sausages. They repeated the seaweed and the food layers until the pit was full. Then they put on a final layer of seaweed, and stretched a tarpaulin over the pile while the hot stones made the seaweed steam, and the food cooked.

Another crew set up a vast striped tent with a pole peak at either end, from which flew Paradise Yacht Club banners. A full bar set up underneath it, and beer kegs chilled in huge tubs of ice. By two-thirty in the afternoon the island was already crowded. People came from the harbor in their own small boats, or were ferried by the Paradise Yacht Club launch. People from town drove over the causeway and parked where they could. A four-man police detail would try to manage the traffic, and later, the clambakers.

Jesse stood beside Hardy Watkins, resting his elbows on the low cabin of the harbor boat, as it idled near the outer harbor. Through the binoculars, Stiles Island was a swarm of tan legs, white shorts, tank tops, big hats, long dresses, pink cotton, blue ribbon, floral patterns, yellow linen. The smell of the bake drifted to him, edged with the smell of fresh spilled beer.

Jesse moved the glasses back to the *Lady Jane*, where a woman came over the side and joined others in the small launch. It might have been Blondie Martin. The launch pulled away from the *Lady Jane* and ran in a big smooth curve toward the Stiles Island dock.

"That's nine," Jesse said. "The boat should be empty."

"You want to come in from the other side," Hardy said.

"Yes."

Hardy opened the throttle gently and the harbor boat moved quietly through the small harbor chop, behind the screen of moored yachts, to the far side of the *Lady*

Jane. He throttled back and let the boat drift in against the side of the yacht, and held it there.

"You see anyone heading for the boat," Jesse said, "give me a shout. If we get caught, I'll lie, and you'll swear to it, that I just went aboard thinking there was someone home, and was about to leave when I found there wasn't."

"We doing something illegal?" Hardy said.

"We are."

"I was hoping it would be something better than this."

Jesse went effortlessly over the side, and onto the deck of the Lady Jane. Away from the low idle of the harbor boat, Jesse heard music coming from Stiles Island. There was no sound on the yacht.

"Hello?" Jesse yelled.

No one answered.

He walked into the cockpit and stopped beside the helm.

"Hello?"

No one answered. He went down the short wide teak stairway. It was a big boat, but there was no extra space. Jesse paused for a moment and yelled once more. No answer. Everything was built-in. Dining table, seating for six, bar, galley, a big plasma television screen, polished hardwood and shiny brass. A small corridor off the back of the dining room had staterooms along either side. Each had a built-in bed and bureau. The master suite had its own head. There were several other facilities tucked in among the staterooms. Jesse counted sleeping for more than nine, though it probably depended somewhat on gender and relationship. Everything looked neat and cozy and expensive and luxurious. The table was set. There were flowers in small crystal vases. Jesse wondered how it was in thirty-five-mile-an-hour winds with a six-foot sea running. The thought made him smile.

The boat was empty. After his walk-through, Jesse began to search each space. He began with the master bedroom. Most people hid the most incriminating stuff, Jesse knew, in their bedroom. Or stateroom, or whatever the swabbies called them.

There were women's clothes and toiletries as well as men's. There were sex toys in the top bureau drawer under some neatly folded sport shirts. One of the toys was a massager which was held onto the back of the hand with springs and imparted its vibration to the hand. Jesse remembered that when he was a small boy in Arizona, his grandfather had used one like it for scalp massage. Jesse smiled. Or maybe not. In the bottom drawer of the same bureau, among a lot of exotic woman's underwear, was a stack of videotapes held together with a thick red elastic band. Jesse picked them up and took off the rubber band. The tapes were numbered with a Magic Marker, but there was nothing else to say what they were. Jesse glanced around the bedroom. In a wall cabinet was an entertainment center which included, Jesse was sure, a videotape player. Jesse studied the equipment. There seemed to be a computer involved. After awhile he shook his head. Defeated by technology.

If I try this, I will fuck it up, and they'll know I was here.

He glanced around the room. He didn't see anything that would help. He went to the closet and opened the bifold doors. The clothes were hung neatly and carefully spaced. Men's and women's. On the top shelf were several long-billed caps and a stack of videotapes. Jesse took them down. They were unmarked, and, he realized, unopened. He went back out and up the stairs to the helm and navigation area, and found a Magic Marker, one of several, in a beer mug on the shelf by the steering wheel.

127

He took it back downstairs, took out the stack of numbered videotapes, slipped one from the middle, number five, took the wrapping cellophane off the new video, marked it number five, slipped it in among the others marked tapes, put the red elastic back around them and put the real number five inside his shirt. He put the other new videos back where he'd found them, crumpled the cellophane that he'd removed and put it in his pocket.

Let's hope it's not his kid's confirmation.

Jesse went through the other rooms, and found a lot that was titillating, but nothing that was useful. Then he went back and sat and looked at the master bedroom. He thought about the tapes. It could all be in there. How hard could it be? He studied the entertainment center.

Okay, this is the remote.

He studied the many buttons. Some had arrows or squares or two bars, or dots. Some were labeled. He found a switch that was labeled ALL ON. He found no other switch that said ALL OFF.

So this must be the one, all on/all off.

He pressed it. The set clicked on, the screen brightened. And in a moment there was a picture. Jesse studied it for a moment. He was looking at a small shower. He clicked the button that read CH. He was looking at a bed. The plaid spread looked familiar.

For Christ's sake. It's on the boat. The bastard's got the place wired.

Jesse stood and walked to the bedroom with the plaid spread. He placed a pillow in the middle of it and went back to the master bedroom. The bed on the screen now had a pillow in the middle of it. Jesse went back, replaced the pillow and stood in the small bedroom looking at the ceiling. There were small recessed lights in the ceiling. Jesse examined them in the low ceiling. He could find nothing unusual. He went back to the master bedroom and clicked the channels. Each shower and each bedroom could be accessed on the screen, including the master bedroom. Jesse went and turned on one of the showers and came back. He could hear it.

Sound and Picture.

He went back and shut off the shower. Then he went to the master bedroom and pressed the all on button. The screen went black. Jesse whistled to himself softly. Master technician!

Has to be through the ceiling lights. The fact that I can't figure it out means nothing. I can't even play the fucking

129

VCR. He put the remote carefully back where he'd found it. He looked around. Everything looked the same as it had.

Jesse went up on deck and over the side onto the harbor boat. Hardy eased it away from the *Lady Jane*, and curled it inconspicuously back in toward the town wharf, moving slowly among the moored sailboats.

25

The videotape player in Jesse's office was simplicity itself. It didn't do anything but play, and required only the ability to push the PLAY and STOP buttons on the remote. Jesse put in tape number five and clicked PLAY.

It was a red-haired woman with slim hips and, Jesse speculated, enhanced breasts. The videotape showed her naked in a variety of activities: taking a shower, shaving her legs, washing her hair, putting on makeup, changing clothes, having various and inventive sex with Harrison Darnell. The tape was a long one and repetitive. Showers, sex, changing clothes, sex, showers, clothes.

Jesse sat quietly at his desk watching. He felt like a dirty old man, alone in a room watching sex videos. It was exciting for about a minute. The pleasures of voyeurism. A moment of discovery. Jesse could not remember seeing a naked redhead before. And then the increasing boredom as the scenes became repetitive. There was sound, but little to listen to, except the sex with Darnell, which was so noisy that Jesse muted it.

Somewhere in the middle of the tape the redhead got a perm. What had been longish wavy hair became short curly hair. Otherwise she continued to shower and change clothes and have sex with Darnell.

The tape ran an hour. The boredom was penetrating. Jesse forced himself to watch it. When it ended he rewound it and sat quietly in his office for a while. He was pretty sure what was on the other tapes. Blondie probably had her own tape. What if tape number five had been Florence Horvath. Then he'd have a choke hold on the son of a bitch. Jesse shook his head. He was guessing. Darnell may not have known Florence Horvath. Florence Horvath might have fallen off the Stiles Island Causeway and drowned. Darnell may have lied just because he didn't want to be bothered. Guys like him would be too busy to be involved in a homicide. Had nude film to watch. Jesse sat for a moment doodling the yellow legal pad on his desktop. Why would Darnell kill Florence? Why would he go to such voyeuristic lengths to get nude movies of women he saw naked regularly? *Sick bastard.*

The door opened a crack and Molly looked in.

"Got some time?"

"Sure," Jesse said.

26

Molly brought in Sam Holton and his wife and daughter.

"You know Sam," Molly said.

"From softball," Jesse said. "Lotta stick, not much foot."

Sam said, "Hi, Jesse."

"This is his wife, Jackie, and his daughter Cathleen. Cathleen says she's been raped."

"I'm sorry," Jesse said.

Cathleen nodded. She was a tall, robust, dark-haired girl with big breasts and long legs. She looked about twenty-five. Her mother was thin and small and pale-skinned, with narrow lips and small eyes which looked bigger behind thick glasses. Nobody said anything.

"Says it happened onboard a yacht named the *Lady Jane*," Molly said.

Thank you, Lord.

"Tell me about it," Jesse said.

"I already told her," Cathleen said.

"Tell me," Jesse said gently.

"Go ahead, Cathleen," her father said.

"Sam, it's embarrassing," Jackie said. "She already told the woman."

Jesse looked at Molly.

"Rape kit?" he said.

"Inconclusive. Signs of penetration, but no semen, no evidence of force."

"You saying I lied," Cathleen said.

"No, honey, inconclusive doesn't mean you lied."

"He wore a rubber," Cathleen said. "Naturally there's no sperm."

"Who?" Jesse said.

"She doesn't know for sure," Molly said. "She thinks it was the boat owner."

Jesse nodded.

"Could you pick him out of a lineup?" Jesse said.

"Absolutely," Cathleen said.

"Good," Jesse said. "How'd you happen to end up on the yacht?"

Cathleen looked down and didn't answer.

"She met one of the crew," Molly said, "at the Dory. He offered to show her the boat."

"How old are you, Cathleen?" Jesse said.

"Seventeen," she said. "I'll be eighteen in September."

"What happened when you got to the boat?" Jesse said.

Cathleen looked irritated.

"I can't talk about stuff like that in front of them," she said.

Sam looked at his hands, folded in his lap. He was a thick man, a landscaper in town. As he got older he'd put on weight but he still looked like someone who'd worked all his life. Jackie glared silently at everyone. Her thin self was tight with anger.

"How about me?" Jesse said.

She looked disgusted.

"No way," she said.

"Okay, then it'll be Molly. Take her to the squad room," Jesse said. "It should be empty. If anyone's in there, give them the boot."

Molly nodded.

Cathleen said, "I don't like talking about it."

"Come on, hon," Molly said. "I'm fun to talk with."

"Yeah, right," Cathleen said. But she stood and followed Molly out.

"She didn't do nothing wrong," Jackie said. Her thin hands were clenched together in her lap.

"I'm sure she didn't," Jesse said.

"Probably shouldn't have gone out to the yacht," Sam said.

"She's a teenager," Jackie said. "They do foolish things."

Sam nodded. His head was down, and he appeared to be studying his thick hands.

"You got to do something about this, Jesse."

Jesse nodded.

"I didn't want to come here. I wanted to get some guys and go out and beat the shit out of everybody on the fucking boat."

"Coming here was better," Jesse said.

"I have to, I'll go out there myself and break the fucking boat up."

"You won't have to," Jesse said.

"She's a good girl," Jackie said. "A little wild, maybe, like most kids. But at heart she's a good girl."

"Anyone can see that," Jesse said.

"She's got a boyfriend. She's going to UMass in the fall."

"This will pass," Jesse said, just as if he meant it.

"And she's underage, isn't she?" Jackie said.

"No, Jackie, she's not. Not if she's seventeen," Jesse said. "Statutory age of consent in this state is sixteen."

"Well, they took advantage of a young girl."

Jesse nodded. Everyone was quiet. Jesse was good at quiet. Silence was his friend.

"Does everyone have to know?" Sam said.

"There might be some publicity, depends mostly on the suspect. If he's not newsworthy, and we stay out of court with a plea bargain, nobody needs to know. I got no need to talk about it."

"You called him a suspect," Jackie said. "You think she's lying?"

Jesse shook his head. "Just cop talk, Jackie. He's a suspect until we convict him."

"Well, she says she was raped, she was raped."

Molly brought Cathleen back.

"I have a full statement," Molly said.

Jesse nodded.

"Anything else you want to say, Cathleen?"

"Nope."

"Okay," Jesse said. "We'll arrange a lineup."

"I'll know the bastard," Cathleen said.

"Cathleen!" Jackie said.

"Well, he is a bastard," Cathleen said.

Sam stood.

"He gets off, Jesse, I swear, I'll deal with him myself," Sam said.

Jesse stood and put out his hand.

"No need, Sam, we're on it."

They all shook hands, and Molly showed them out. Jesse thought that Cathleen's handshake was not enthusiastic.

27

When Molly came back into Jesse's office, Jesse was looking out his window at the fire trucks being washed on the firehouse driveway beneath his window. He liked the way the stream of water from the hose sluiced away the suds worked up by the sponge. He liked the way it slid smoothly off and as the water dried up, the red finish of the truck gleamed in the morning sun.

"Rape, my ass," Molly said.

Jesse nodded. Outside the firemen began to polish the chrome. They liked that truck. *Like grooming a horse,* Jesse thought. *If it was alive, they'd give it a carrot.*

"Let's hear her statement," Jesse said.

Molly got the audiotape of her interview with Cathleen and they listened to it in Jesse's office.

"They made me do a striptease," Cathleen said.

"What were the circumstances?" Molly asked.

"They got a video camera, and they said

I had to do a striptease or they wouldn't take me home."

"Who is they?" Molly said.

"The guy that raped me and other guys and some women, too. They said I had to strip."

"Perfect," Jesse said.

"Keep listening," Molly said.

"And then the guy who owned the boat took me into his bedroom and closed the door and threw me on the bed and raped me. He was like an animal. Just threw me down and jumped on me and stuck it in."

"But, he did wear a condom," Molly said.

"Yeah, sure."

"Did he put that on just before he jumped on you like an animal?"

"Yeah, just before."

"Was it in a packet?" Molly said. *"Did he have to open the packet?"*

"No, he just . . . he had it in his pocket and just pulled it out and put it on."

They listened to the rest of it. She might have had a drink, but if she did, it was only one and she didn't finish it. What kind of drink? Vodka. Straight? Yes. Who brought her home? Same guy brought her out. The one she met in the bar. Could she pick him out of a lineup? Yeah, 'course.

When the tape was finished, Jesse said, "She got drunk at the Dory, went on a lark to the yacht. They fed her more booze. She got drunker and did a striptease. Then the owner brought her into his bedroom and had sex with her. They brought her home. Maybe they didn't treat her respectfully. Maybe she just was in trouble at home for being late and being drunk. Maybe she was afraid the tape they made of her striptease would get out. Whatever, she came up with this story."

Molly nodded.

"Her mother knows she wasn't raped," Molly said.

"Yes," Jesse said. "She does."

"I guess Sam believes her. I hope he doesn't do something about this that will get him in trouble."

"He'll let us do our thing," Jesse said. "He's like a lot of fathers in this situation. He's saying what he thinks he's supposed to say."

"What are you going to do?"

Jesse smiled.

"We don't know she's making this up," Jesse said.

"We're pretty sure," Molly said.

"It's not our job to decide," Jesse said. "It's our job to investigate. The DA and the courts decide."

"If we got her in here alone and talked to her for a while," Molly said, "she'd tell us she's lying."

"We don't want to do that," Jesse said.

"We don't?"

"Then we'd have no reason to search the alleged crime scene."

"The *Lady Jane*?" Molly said.

"And confiscate any videotape we might find," Jesse said.

Molly began to nod her head slowly.

"And since it is a lawful search, if we stumbled across anything that looked like evidence in the Florence Horvath homicide . . ." she said.

"Sometimes it's better to be lucky than good," Jesse said.

"It helps to know what to do with the luck when it comes your way," Molly said.

"Yes, it does," Jesse said.

28

Kelly Cruz sat on a terrace in the tallest building south of New York and looked at Biscayne Bay. The Cuban maid brought her iced tea with mint.

"Mister and Missus will come right out, soon," the maid said.

Kelly Cruz nodded. The maid backed off the terrace. Kelly Cruz watched an ornate white cruise ship plod fatly south in the bay. She had never been on a cruise, but she couldn't imagine it was much fun.

"Miss Cruz? Nice to see you again."

Kelly Cruz put her tea down and stood.

"Mr. Plum," she said. "Mrs. Plum."

Everyone shook hands.

"Sit down," Mr. Plum said, "please."

The Cuban maid appeared with iced tea for the Plums.

"That will be all, Magdalena," Mrs. Plum said. "Thank you."

The first time she'd met them, Kelly Cruz thought they looked like brother and sister. Mrs. Plum had thick silver hair brushed back, and very large sunglasses.

Her skin was evenly tanned. She was slim and wearing a white silk shirt with white linen slacks and sandals. Her toenails were polished. Early sixties, Kelly Cruz estimated. Both of them. Mr. Plum looked like his wife. Silvery hair, brushed back, even tan, dark glasses, white shirt and slacks. Mr. Plum smiled at Kelly Cruz.

"Did I tell you when you came by last time?" he said. "That you're quite attractive for a detective."

"It's a disguise," Kelly Cruz said.

Mr. Plum smiled widely and nodded in a way that made Kelly Cruz think he hadn't understood what she said.

"Do you have any new information about Florence's death," Mrs. Plum said.

"I need to ask you some more questions, tell you some things we have learned," Kelly Cruz said, "and get your comments. Not all of the things will be pleasant."

"Must you?" Mrs. Plum said. "Don't you think we may have heard enough unpleasant things?"

"She has to do her job, Mommy," Mr. Plum said.

"Do you know a man named Thomas Ralston?" Kelly Cruz said.

Mr. Plum looked thoughtful for a time. Then he said, "No, I'm afraid I don't."

"Mrs. Plum?" Kelly Cruz said.

"He's one of the crowd of pimps and gigolos that Florence knew."

"Florence? Are you sure, Mommy? I don't remember him."

"You remember only what you want to," Mrs. Plum said. "And I'm not your mother."

Mr. Plum smiled at his wife.

"Which was he," Kelly Cruz said.

"I don't know. He had money. He owned a yacht. That was enough for Florence."

"How did he get his money?"

"Wise choice of parents," Mrs. Plum said. "Or, more likely, grandparents."

She glanced briefly at her husband. Perhaps he wasn't a self-made man, either, Kelly Cruz thought. He smiled happily at his wife.

"How well do you know him."

"I've met him once or twice."

"So you don't know him well?"

"To know him at all is to know him too well."

"He doesn't seem like a bad sort, Mommy," Mr. Plum said.

"I thought you didn't know him," Kelly Cruz said.

"Mommy, Mrs. Plum, reminded me," he said.

Kelly Cruz nodded.

"Any thoughts?" Kelly Cruz said.

"Me?" Mr. Plum said. "No. As I said, he seemed nice."

"Where did you meet him."

Mr. Plum looked blank. Mrs. Plum said, "Tennis club luau. Florence brought a bunch of people. We didn't even know she'd be there."

"Would you have gone if you'd known?"

"No."

"Do you know where I could find Mr. Ralston?"

"I believe he lives aboard his boat," Mrs. Plum said.

"In Fort Lauderdale?"

"He never said."

Kelly Cruz nodded. She knew that Mr. Ralston's boat was currently in Paradise, Massachusetts.

"We have in our possession," Kelly Cruz said, "a videotape of Florence having sex with two men."

Mrs. Plum squeezed her eyes tight shut and dropped her head. Mr. Plum looked faintly quizzical. Neither of them spoke.

"I'm sorry," Kelly Cruz said. "Do you know anything about that?"

"Well," Mr. Plum said, with a pleasant smile, "Florence was sort of wild, I guess."

"Mrs. Plum?" Kelly Cruz said.

Mrs. Plum hadn't moved. She appeared to be staring at her knees.

"I'm not surprised," she said without looking up.

"Would you know what the circumstances would be that would . . ." Kelly Cruz stopped.

"Cause her to do something like that?" Mrs. Plum said. "Too much money, too much freedom, too little supervision . . . too little love."

"But you don't know of any, ah, commercial enterprise that she might have been involved with?"

"Oh my God, no," Mrs. Plum said. "Nothing that smacked of work. She would have done it because it was shocking, or depraved, or unconventional. Maybe because she thought it was fun. But never work. Never anything as worthwhile as commercial enterprise."

Mr. Plum seemed to have lost interest.

"It's not an investigative question, Mrs. Plum, but I have two children, and . . ."

"And you can't imagine giving up on them so completely."

"Did you love her?"

"Yes, I did. God save me, I do. But I had to make choices. I have two other daugh-

147

ters, much younger. I couldn't let her corrupt them as she had been corrupted."

"By whom," Kelly Cruz said.

Still staring down at her knees with her eyes shut, Mrs. Plum said, "See above."

"Too much freedom, too little love?" Kelly Cruz said.

Mrs. Plum nodded. Mr. Plum was looking at his watch.

"You know, it's after five somewhere," he said.

He picked up a small silver bell and rang it. The maid appeared.

"I'm going to order drinks," Mr. Plum said. "What's your pleasure, Miss Cruz."

Kelly Cruz shook her head.

"I'm working," she said.

Mr. Plum nodded.

"Two old-fashioneds, Magdalena," he said. "Tell Felix to be sure and use those lowball glasses I like. He knows."

Magdalena nodded and went out.

Kelly Cruz took a deep breath.

"Your twin daughters," she said. "They aren't in Europe."

Mrs. Plum's shoulders rose and fell as she breathed deeply.

"They are not students at Emory University."

No one said anything. From under Mrs.

148

Plum's closed eyelids, a couple of tears began to slip down her face. Mr. Plum looked puzzled. He glanced hopefully toward the patio door.

"Did you know that," Kelly Cruz said, "when I talked with you last time?"

Mrs. Plum nodded.

"Why did you lie?"

"I . . . I knew they had dropped out and I didn't know where they had gone."

"Why'd you lie?"

"What kind of a mother doesn't even know where her kids are?" Mrs. Plum said.

The maid came in and put an old-fashioned next to Mrs. Plum. Mr. Plum took his from her hand and drank some. He smiled and exhaled audibly. Mrs. Plum opened her wet eyes and looked at the drink which was already beginning to bead moisture in the warmth of the terrace.

"Oh God," she said, and picked up her glass.

29

"So how come I get to go on this big search," Molly said. "There women involved?"

"There's some women," Jesse said.

They were on the harbor boat.

"Otherwise you and Suit would have done it yourselves."

"Nice to have a woman, in an isolated situation, where there are other women."

"So I'm like the nurse in the examining room."

"Exactly," Jesse said.

"How come I never get to do guy cop things."

Jesse shrugged.

"Next time Carl Radborn gets drunk in the Dory we'll give you a shout," he said.

Molly grinned.

"Women are nice," she said.

Hardy pulled the boat in alongside the *Lady Jane*, and held it there while the three cops went aboard.

"Be awhile, Hardy," Jesse said. "I'll call you on the cell phone."

"I'll lay off here a little to the leeward," Hardy said. "No hurry."

"Leeward," Suitcase said.

"I love it," Molly said, "when you talk salty."

Hardy didn't respond and the three cops scrambled up onto the deck of the *Lady Jane*.

Harrison Darnell met them himself. His guests were gathered at breakfast. The crew, except for the captain, was serving. There were bagels and muffins. There was cheese and a platter of fruit, coffee and a pitcher of orange juice. A bottle of champagne stood in a bucket. Blondie was drinking a Bloody Mary.

"What is it now?" Darnell said.

He was in shorts and boat shoes and a flowered shirt. Jesse handed him the warrant.

"A crime has been alleged on board," Jesse said. "That's a warrant to search the boat."

"Crime?"

"A young woman alleges rape."

"Rape? For crissake, Stone, I don't have to rape anyone."

"We will also require that you not leave the harbor, and that you come in for a lineup."

"Lineup?" Darnell said. "What the fuck

151

are you talking about. A fucking lineup?"

Jesse nodded enthusiastically.

"Yes," Jesse said, "that's what it's often called."

"You have no damned jurisdiction here," Darnell said. "We're at sea."

"You're in Paradise Harbor, Mr. Darnell," Jesse said. "Why don't you sit down over there, have a nice cup of tea or something."

"I want a lawyer."

Jesse shrugged.

"Call one," he said. "Officer Crane and I will search the ship. Officer Simpson will stay with you on deck."

"I won't allow it," Darnell said. "It is a travesty. There has been no crime. Ask anyone."

He stepped in front of the stairwell.

"You are not going below."

"Of course we are, Mr. Darnell," Jesse said. "It's just a question of hard or easy."

"What's hard?" Blondie Martin asked from her seat at the table. Her eyes were wide and full of excitement as she looked at Jesse over the rim of her glass.

"Easy is Mr. Darnell goes and sits down with you," Jesse said. "Step aside, Mr. Darnell."

There was something frantic in Darnell's resistance.

"No," he said. "You aren't going below."

Jesse took the cuffs off his belt.

"You are under arrest, Mr. Darnell, for refusing a lawful order. Face the bulkhead, please. Hands on the top."

Darnell's voice slid up into a high vibrato.

"No," he said. "No."

Jesse took hold of Darnell's right forearm. Darnell tried to pull away, Jesse started to turn him, and Darnell swung at Jesse with his left hand. Jesse avoided the punch, used the momentum it generated to spin Darnell, slammed him against the bulkhead and pinned him there with his shoulder while he snapped the cuff on his right wrist. Darnell flailed with his left hand, but Jesse caught it, brought it down and clicked onto the left wrist. It was all so quick, Darnell had no chance to stabilize himself for a real resistance.

Blondie said, "Ooooh!"

Jesse let Darnell away from the bulkhead.

"Suit, sit him down somewhere, and keep him there," Jesse said.

"Boy, Chief Yokel," Blondie said. "You're really quick."

"Maybe Mr. Darnell is really slow," Jesse said.

"Any time you want to play with your

handcuffs . . ." Blondie said and giggled.

Jesse heard Molly make a small sound.

"First we'll search the boat," Jesse said.

He and Molly started down the stairs.

"Did I hear you snicker, Officer Crane?" Jesse said.

"You might have, Chief Yokel," Molly said, laughter bubbling beneath her voice.

"Well, as long as it was a respectful snicker," Jesse said.

"Absolutely," Molly said.

Wearing gloves and carrying evidence bags, they went stateroom to stateroom together. Jesse never split a search. It was Jesse's view that two people searching the same room made it less likely that either would miss something. The videotapes were right where Jesse had left them. There were two more. He took the tapes, including the empty substitute that he had substituted, so everything would look kosher.

"There is a selection of controlled substances here," Molly said. "Some weed. Some, I assume, coke. Couple of other things I'd need help with."

"Pack it up," Jesse said.

"We going to arrest them for possession?"

"I might find it useful as leverage," Jesse said.

In the night table of the master cabin, Jesse

found a Browning Hi-Power and a box of shells. He took the pistol and left the shells. In the crew quarters he found a shotgun. He left it. Most boats had a long gun aboard. He didn't think it would do much for him. They confiscated a video camera. They found sex toys in most of the staterooms. There were several vibrators, some anatomically correct. Molly turned one over in her hands, looking at it from all angles.

"When I was in parochial school," Molly said, "we weren't allowed to wear patent leather shoes, for fear someone might look up our dress in the reflection."

"I was always hopeful about that," Jesse said. "But I never saw it work."

"But it probably kept you alert," Molly said.

"I don't want you sneaking home with that thing," Jesse said.

Molly rolled her eyes at him, and put the vibrator back where she found it.

"Ah, the stories it could tell," he said.

"What exactly is this," Molly said.

"That's a ball gag," Jesse said, "and those are restraints. Fetish toys. You can order them on the Internet."

"Ick," Molly said.

"You and hubby don't use those?" Jesse said.

"There are times, I think, he might want to stick that gag in my mouth," Molly said. "But not during sex."

"Irish Catholic girls have sex?" Jesse said.

"When we go bad," Molly said, "we go way bad."

When they were through the search it was midway through the afternoon. Jesse made an inventory of what they'd confiscated, in duplicate, and signed it. Then he called Hardy on the cell phone.

"What did you take?" Darnell said, when they reached the deck.

"Stuff," Jesse said. "Uncuff him, Suit."

Simpson unlocked the cuffs on Darnell. Jesse separated the two sheets of his inventory and handed the carbon sheet to Darnell.

"You can't take the tapes. They're private property."

"We'll need you to come in and do a lineup," Jesse said. "All of you. Crew as well. We'll arrange a date and get back to you."

"Those tapes aren't even mine. Somebody left them on board. I don't even know what's on them."

"We'll take a look, let you know. Meanwhile, if you leave the harbor I'll have the

Coast Guard impound the boat."

"I want a lawyer," Darnell said.

"Sure, when you get one, tell him you are suspected of forcible rape. In fact, all of you are suspects."

"Those aren't my tapes," Darnell said again.

"Have a swell day," Jesse said, and waited at the rail while Molly climbed down to join Suit in the harbor boat.

"Can the Coast Guard impound his boat?" Molly said as they headed back through the moored boats toward the town pier.

"I don't know," Jesse said. "I probably ought to ask somebody."

30

Kelly Cruz sat at the bar of the Boat Club, at the marina, near the causeway in Fort Lauderdale, sipping a Diet Coke. The bartender was maybe twenty-two, and red-haired. He wore small blue oval sunglasses with blue lenses. He had on big shorts and a white tee shirt that said BIG RED on the front. There was some sort of choker around his neck.

"Why you wanna know about Mr. Ralston?" the bartender said.

"What is your name?" Kelly Cruz said.

"Brick," he said.

"I'm Kelly Cruz," she said, and showed him her badge. "Tell me about Mr. Ralston."

"You're a cop?"

"I am."

"What'd he do?"

"I understand he lives on his boat in this marina," Kelly Cruz said.

"I don't know where he lives," Brick said. "But he's in here a lot."

"Seen him lately?"

"No, I think he went up north to some boat racing thing."

"You remember all your customers?" Kelly Cruz said.

"The ones tip like Mr. Ralston," Brick said. "Plus he's a really cool dude, you know. I mean, no offense, but he comes in here with some of the most bodacious-looking women, hoo hah!"

"Hoo hah?" Kelly Cruz said.

"You know," Brick said, "bada-bing! Excellent."

The bar was mostly empty. There were a few people scattered at tables in the glass-walled room with the turquoise light from the ocean coming in on two sides. Outside on the deck, several other tables were occupied. A waitress moved among them with her tray.

"Know any of them?"

"The babes that hang with Mr. Ralston? Just to say s'happenin'."

"Are any of these women here now?"

"No."

"Does Mr. Ralston have anyone, like, steady?"

"Naw," Brick said. "Guy like that doesn't do steady. He just hooks up, you know? Blonde one night, brunette the next. No flames, no games. No hellos, no goodbyes. No aches, no pains. Just slam bam alakazam."

Brick grinned.

"You admire Mr. Ralston," Kelly Cruz said.

"You bet. He's leading my life, instead of me."

Brick slid a saucer of mixed nuts within Kelly Cruz's reach.

"But I'll get there."

"Everybody needs a dream," Kelly Cruz said.

"Want me to freshen up that DC?" Brick said. "Wedge of lime, anything?"

Kelly Cruz shook her head.

"Know what Mr. Ralston does for a living?"

Brick grinned wider.

"I think it's maybe just slam bam alakazam," he said.

"You ever been on his boat?"

"I have, in point of actual fact," Brick said. "Worked a private party for him one night, tending bar. That was tough, baby. That was an absolute groove."

"Wild party?" Kelly Cruz said.

"I mean, I don't want to cause anybody any trouble," he said.

"Just gathering information," Kelly Cruz said. "I don't care if there was a little blow being snorted."

"Blow? Yeah, I guess so, and booze, and mara-joo-wanna, sure. But it was the sex thing, man, everybody doing everything with everybody and the video cameras rolling, and . . . whew! I was afraid for a time there, I was going to lose my cherry."

He smiled broadly.

"Know any of the people on the boat?" Kelly Cruz said.

"Not really, you know, 'hi, howya doin'. But Courtney does."

"Courtney," Kelly Cruz said.

"The waitress," Brick said. "Right over there. I know she hangs with one of Mr. Ralston's girls. You wanna talk with her?"

"I do," Kelly Cruz said.

"Hey, Court," Brick said. "Come talk to the nice lady for a minute."

The waitress came to the bar.

"I got half a dozen tables, you idiot," she said to Brick.

"Nobody's at the bar," Brick said. "They need something I'll cover it."

Courtney frowned. Her face was so blank that the frown looked as if it had hurt to perform.

"No offense, ma'am. How can I help you?"

Kelly Cruz showed her badge.

"Kelly Cruz," she said.

Courtney said, "Yes, ma'am."

"Call me Kelly. Just a couple of girls gossiping."

"Yes, ma'am."

"You know Thomas Ralston?" Kelly Cruz said.

"Mr. Ralston?"

"Un-huh."

"Everybody knows him," Courtney said. "He comes here a lot."

"Do you know any of his, ah, girls."

"His girls?"

"I heard," Kelly Cruz said, "you hung with one of Mr. Ralston's girls."

Courtney made her frown face again, and looked at Brick. He grinned at her.

"You know, Court, the one with all the hair," he said. "Mandy."

Kelly Cruz looked at Courtney and waited.

"Mandy," Courtney said. "Yo, I know Mandy."

"And she's, ah, friendly with Thomas Ralston?" Kelly Cruz said.

Courtney looked back at the tables she was waitressing. No one was looking for her. She looked at Brick. He smiled and shrugged.

"She dates him sometimes," Courtney said after a time.

"Un-huh," Kelly Cruz said. "You ever date him?"

"Me? Oh, God no. I'm in college."

"Mr. Ralston doesn't date college girls?"

Courtney struggled with her face. Kelly Cruz waited.

"No . . . I don't know," Courtney said. "I'm not the kind of girl he dates is what I mean."

"What kind of girl does he date?"

"Not like me," Courtney said. "He's been around too much, you know? I like guys my own age. He's too . . . he's too sexy."

Kelly Cruz nodded.

"I'd like to get in touch with Mandy. Could you give me her address, please."

"I don't want to get her in trouble," Courtney said.

Kelly Cruz nodded.

"I'll need the address, Courtney."

"Do I have to?"

"Yes, honey," Kelly Cruz said, "you do."

31

"I can't watch those tapes with Molly," Suitcase Simpson said.

"I'm all right with it, Suit," Molly said.

"I'm not," Suit said. "I'd be too embarrassed."

"Okay," Jesse said. "No need. If you have to see them you can watch later on your own."

Molly and Jesse watched the tapes. They were predictably repetitive: sex, showers, changing clothes. One tape was of Cathleen Holton doing a drunken clumsy embarrassing strip on the deck. The tape continued with her having sex with Darnell, during which she was clearly willing, in fact eager, and clearly inept.

"Oh God," Molly said, watching Cathleen. "The poor thing."

Jesse nodded. The tapes ground on. Many women. Several no older than Cathleen Holton. Jesse counted five other men besides Darnell. Two of them Jesse had seen aboard the *Lady Jane.* He wondered if the men knew they'd been videotaped.

"There's no bathroom stuff," Jesse said.

"Just the showers," Molly said.

"Doesn't fit the fantasy," Jesse said.

"I guess not," Molly said.

On the screen another young girl was climbing into bed with Darnell.

"Jesus Christ," Molly said.

Jesse froze the frame.

"I know her," Molly said.

"Local girl," Jesse said.

"Katie, Kate DeWolfe. She's in school with my oldest."

"Which would make her how old?" Jesse said.

"Fifteen."

"Under age."

Molly nodded. They both stared at the frozen image of the girl.

"Which gives us another handhold on Darnell," she said.

"Doesn't prove he killed Florence Horvath," Jesse said.

"Proves he's a bad man," Molly said.

"We knew that."

"What in God's name will I tell her mother?" Molly said.

Jesse didn't say anything. They both looked at Katie DeWolfe for another moment. Then Jesse pressed play, and the videotape unspooled relentlessly. The tapes seemed infinite. Blondie Martin took her turn. They watched all day and when it was over had not seen Florence Horvath.

They sat silently when the last scene had played and the last tape had rewound. There was nothing to say. They didn't look at each other.

"I may never have sex again," Molly said after a time.

"I know," Jesse said.

"You've probably seen worse," Molly said.

"Yes."

"But . . ."

"It's the quantity," Jesse said.

"Yes," Molly said. "That's what it is. The women become interchangeable. They are just parts. Nipples and pubic hair. There's no . . . there's no . . ."

Molly stopped and shook her head.

"Humanity," Jesse said.

"Yes. Nothing human is happening. Do men find this exciting?"

"I don't," Jesse said.

"Not for a minute?"

"First ten seconds, maybe," Jesse said. "More anticipation, probably, than anything."

"Those tapes shouldn't exist," Molly said. "Am I a prude?"

"We had to watch it," Jesse said. "Not everybody does."

"So you're saying it should exist."

"Most people, I'd say if you don't like it, don't look at it."

"It's worse than that," Molly said. "I don't want it available to anyone who wants to look."

"Not my area," Jesse said. "But my guess is that it would probably do more harm to try and prevent it."

"Censorship and all that," Molly said.

"I don't mind censorship," Jesse said, "long as I get to be censor."

Molly smiled.

"Yes. I know. But damn . . ."

"Consenting adults," Jesse said.

"Not all of them," Molly said.

Jesse smiled.

"There's that," he said.

32

Kelly Cruz sat with Mandy Morello at an outdoor table outside a bakery and deli near the Marriott Marina Hotel. Kelly Cruz was drinking coffee. Mandy was having a Pepsi-Cola and eating some sort of napoleon and smoking a cigarette.

"Is sex against the law?" Mandy said.

"Not for consenting adults."

"How about posing for nude pictures?"

"Not for consenting adults."

"Okay," Mandy said. "What would you like to know?"

"Does being one of Mr. Ralston's girls involve sex and nude pictures?" Kelly Cruz said.

"Sure," Mandy said.

She wiped whipped cream off her upper lip.

"Tell me about that," Kelly Cruz said.

"That give you a charge?" Mandy said. "Hearing about it?"

Kelly Cruz sighed.

"Mandy," she said. "I'm a fun person, just like you, but I am also a cop investigating a homicide, and I would just as soon not fuck around with it too much, okay?"

"Whoa," Mandy said. "Kelly, I didn't mean anything. It's just how I talk."

"Sure," Kelly Cruz said. "Tell me about life with Thomas Ralston."

"Well, ah, what can I tell you. He parties."

"With you?"

"Sometimes with me."

"Sometimes with others?"

"Sure."

"One at a time?" Kelly Cruz said.

Mandy rolled her eyes and laughed.

"Not always," she said.

"Other men involved?"

"Sometimes."

"Are we talking about gang bangs here, Mandy?"

"Sometimes."

"Willing?"

"Willing? Oh, sure, willing. Of course, it's all in fun. Somebody doesn't groove on that. Fine. Don't party. You know?"

"What about the nude pictures."

"Oh those," Mandy laughed and stubbed her cigarette out in the remains of her napoleon. "Tommy got it all rigged on his boat, cameras in the bedrooms, all hooked to a VCR."

"Do the participants know they're being

taped?" Kelly Cruz said.

Mandy shrugged.

"I know," she said, "because he showed me some pictures of me."

"You didn't mind?"

"Hell, no, fun stuff. I thought it was cool."

"How'd you meet Mr. Ralston?" Kelly Cruz said.

"Around. I like yachts and men who own them," Mandy said. "You hang around the right marinas and you get to see a lot of both."

"And the other women?" Kelly Cruz said.

Mandy laughed.

"I'm not there," she said, "because I'm interested in the other women."

"Any names?"

"No. I don't know any of them. There's some babe named Brittany, and somebody named Janine, but I don't know any last names."

"Men?"

"Harry," Mandy said with a big smile, "and Mike and a guy named Ace."

"No last names," Kelly Cruz said.

"We're real informal on the yacht," Mandy said.

"You know what Mr. Ralston does with all his videotapes?"

"He looks at them, I guess, in his spare time."

Kelly Cruz nodded.

"Do you know where he is now?" Kelly Cruz said.

Mandy tipped her glass so that the small chunks of ice in the bottom slid into her mouth. She crunched them thoughtfully, and shook her head.

"He's up north near Boston someplace," she said after she swallowed. "There's some big race thing going on."

"Do you know when he'll be back?" Kelly Cruz said.

Mandy shrugged and shook her head.

"Do you know anyone named Florence Horvath?" Kelly Cruz said.

"There was a Florence, hung with Tommy for a while."

"Know anything about her?"

"She was old for Tommy."

"Anything else?"

"No."

"Know where she is now?" Kelly Cruz said.

"No."

"Know any other friends of hers?"

"No."

"Do you know Corliss and Claudia Plum?"

"Twins?" Mandy said.

"Yes."

"Corliss and Claudia, yeah. They been on the boat with Tommy, pretty sure. I mean how many twins you meet, let alone named Claudia and Corliss. Yikes."

"They party with Tommy too?"

"Absolutely. College cuties, you know."

Kelly Cruz took out the three head shots Jesse had sent.

"Know any of these?" she said to Mandy.

Mandy studied the pictures.

"I mighta seen them around the marina, hard to say. Pictures aren't really great, you know?"

"I know," Kelly Cruz said.

Mandy looked some more.

"I can't tell," she said. "Everybody hangs around the marina looks the same, tan, blond. Boys, girls, doesn't matter. Hard to remember."

Kelly Cruz nodded and took the pictures back. She took a card out of her purse and handed it to Mandy.

"Anything occurs to you, call me."

"Sure," Mandy said and tucked the card into her bra.

"Tommy give you money?" Kelly Cruz said.

"He helps out, bless his horny little heart."

"So what are you doing now," Kelly Cruz said, "while Tommy's away?"

Mandy paused to light a new cigarette. "I have other friends," she said.

33

"I been working my little butt off for you down here," Kelly Cruz said on the phone.

"Glad to know it's little," Jesse said.

"Perky, too," Kelly Cruz said.

"Even better," Jesse said. "What do you know."

"I talked to the vic's parents," Kelly Cruz said. "The old man is off in happy land someplace. Booze, denial, Alzheimer's, I don't know. But as far as he knows, everything is dandy and let's have a cocktail."

"How about the mother?"

"She knows. And she doesn't know what to do with it, and so she pretends she doesn't know, and let's have a cocktail."

"She know the twins aren't in school?"

"Yes," Kelly Cruz said. "I feel kind of bad for her."

"She know anything else?"

"She knows that Florence was pals with Thomas Ralston."

"Son of a gun!" Jesse said.

"And the twins," Kelly Cruz said,

"Corliss and Claudia, were also pals with Thomas Ralston."

"You got that from the mother too?"

"No. I did some follow-up," Kelly Cruz said. "I'm trying to make sergeant."

"Follow-up *and* a perky little butt," Jesse said. "You're a lock."

"Yeah. Ralston led a pretty lively sex life. You want to hear?"

"I do," Jesse said.

Kelly Cruz told him everything she'd learned. Jesse listened silently. When she was through he told her what he knew about Harrison Darnell.

"And Darnell's parked right beside Ralston?" Kelly Cruz said.

"In the same harbor," Jesse said. "And, I don't think they call it parked. I think it's anchored, or moored, maybe."

"I'll make a note," Kelly Cruz said. "So they both knew Florence Horvath. They both have the same, ah, atypical sexual interests. And they were both . . . anchored . . . in Paradise Harbor when Florence washed ashore."

"Yes," Jesse said. "Does that seem significant to you?"

"I might check it out, I was you," Kelly Cruz said.

"Thanks," Jesse said.

175

"You're welcome, but there's one other thing, maybe," Kelly Cruz said. "One of the people I talked with down here, a girl, maybe twenty-one, twenty-two, mentioned that Florence Horvath seemed a little old for Thomas Ralston."

"She was thirty-four," Jesse said.

"No accounting for taste," Kelly Cruz said. "Maybe he passed her on to Darnell."

"Darnell seems somewhat able to tolerate age diversity," Jesse said.

"I'll keep snooping around when I'm not busy with my real job," Kelly Cruz said.

When she hung up Jesse sat silently, looking at nothing. The scientists had established that all the tapes were recent. He wondered who the redhead was. He hadn't seen her on Darnell's yacht. There were several he hadn't seen. He had to talk with Katie DeWolfe. And her mother. He couldn't let it slide. She was fifteen. Her mother had to know, too. Molly hadn't mentioned a father. Sometimes he thought the fathers were harder. *Maybe just because I'm male.* He'd have Molly sit in. She knew the mother. When he sat at his desk, Jesse was more comfortable when he took the gun off his hip and laid it on the desktop. He looked at it now, lying there. Be simpler if they would let him just shoot

people who deserved it. *Who would decide?
I would. What if you're wrong? Ah, there's
the rub.*

He stood and went out to the desk.

"Can you arrange for Katie DeWolfe and
her parents to come see me?" he said.

"Father's not around," Molly said.
"They're divorced."

Jesse nodded.

"I should be the one," Molly said. "I
know Katie, and I know her mother."

Jesse nodded again.

"You're going to ask me to sit in, too,"
Molly said. "Aren't you."

Jesse continued to nod. Molly stared
past him for a moment. Then she breathed
in audibly.

"Any special time?" she said.

"Soon as they can," Jesse said. "But, you
know, try to accommodate to them. I'll be
available."

Molly continued to stare at nothing.
Jesse could hear her breathing.

"I wish you could do it," Molly said.

"I can. But I thought it might be more
comfortable for them if you did."

"It will be," Molly said.

Jesse nodded.

"This is not going to be fun," Molly said.

"I never promised you fun."

34

Katie DeWolfe was scared. Her small face was pinched with it. She walked stiffly and swallowed frequently. Her mother had the same look. They looked alike. They were both slender, and blond, and had about them a look of furtive sexuality. Jesse could never quite pin down what the look was. But he always knew it when he saw it, and in those instances when he'd had occasion to test it, he had always been right.

Molly brought them both in, introduced everyone, got the DeWolfes seated, facing the desk, and sat herself in a straight chair crowded in to Jesse's left.

"Do you know what this is about, Katie?" Jesse said.

Katie shook her head.

"You're sure?" Jesse said.

"I got no idea," Katie said.

Jesse nodded and took a breath.

"Okay," he said. "There's no easy way to say it. I have a videotape of you having sex with a man named Harrison Darnell."

"You're lying," Katie said. "It's not me."

"No, honey," Jesse said. "It's you."

Mrs. DeWolfe said in a strangled voice, "Katie?"

"No way," Katie said.

"I can play the tape," Jesse said.

"It's not me."

Jesse nodded. He picked up the remote from his desk and aimed it and clicked and the tape began to roll with a closeup of Katie's face, looking straight up at the camera over a man's shoulder. Katie dropped her head and closed her eyes. Her mother stared at the tape. The camera pulled back to show the two of them naked and copulating.

"Stop it," Mrs. DeWolfe said. "For Christ's sake, stop it."

Jesse clicked the tape off.

"She's fifteen," Mrs. DeWolfe said.

"I know," Jesse said.

Mrs. DeWolfe looked at Molly.

"Molly, for crissake," she said, "what am I supposed to do?"

"If Katie cooperates," Molly said, "we can probably work something out?"

"Cooperates?" Katie said. "I didn't do nothing wrong."

"No," Jesse said. "But he did."

"I'm not ratting Harrison out," she said. "No way. No way."

Mrs. DeWolfe said, "Katie, my God."

"Oh, like you're so lily pure. You been oinkin' a different guy every week since Daddy left."

"Katie, that's not true. And if it were, it doesn't mean you should. I'm a grown woman, for God's sake."

"So am I," Katie said.

She stuck her chest out, so that her small breasts pushed against her cotton tank top.

"You seen the movies."

Her mother slapped her across the face. Katie slapped back at her and her mother gripped her wrists and they grappled there, still seated. Jesse put his head back against the back of his swivel chair and closed his eyes for a moment.

"Molly," he said.

But Molly was already up and separating the two women. Jesse opened his eyes.

"Who's on the desk?" he said.

"Arthur," Molly said.

Jesse picked up the phone and called the desk.

"Arthur," he said. "Step into my office for a moment."

He hung up and the door opened and Arthur Angstrom stood there.

"Take Mrs. DeWolfe out to the front," Jesse said. "Get her seated and be sure she stays there until I holler."

"Okay, Jesse."

"I'm not going anywhere," Mrs. DeWolfe said.

"You are, ma'am," Jesse said. "Easy? Or hard?"

She lingered for a minute but Jesse could tell her heart wasn't in it and she stood.

"I'll be right outside," she said to her daughter.

Arthur took her arm and they went out. Molly closed the office door. Jesse leaned back in his chair and looked at Katie. She looked back at him, trying for defiance.

"So?" she said.

Jesse smiled.

"So," he said.

"Like you never had sex?"

"I'm proud to say I did have sex, and hope to again," Jesse said.

"So, you think I'm too young?"

"Probably," Jesse said.

"You never had sex when you was my age?"

"No," Jesse grinned again. "But it wasn't for lack of trying."

"Everybody my age has had sex," she said.

"Probably not all of them with a stranger forty years older, in front of a video camera," Jesse said.

"Turn you on?" she said.

She looked at him with her eyes wide open. Jesse looked back. *Big, blue, innocent and stupid,* he thought.

"You were maybe the twenty-fifth person I looked at," Jesse said. "I was a long way past turning on."

"So, you gonna arrest me, or what?"

"I don't quite know what to do with you, Katie. Let's try talking about things, just sort of pleasantly. I won't be a tough guy, and you won't be a sexpot, and we'll see where the conversation takes us."

She frowned, trying to puzzle out what he had said.

"You married?"

"Divorced," Jesse said.

"Got a girlfriend?"

Jesse smiled. "Actually, I'm living with my ex-wife," he said.

"That's weird."

Jesse continued to smile.

"Yes," he said. "It certainly is."

"If you're divorced, how come you live together."

"It has to do with love," Jesse said.

"You love her?"

"I think we love each other," Jesse said.

"So how come you got divorced?"

"Long answer," Jesse said. "The short version is, we had problems we couldn't solve."

"And now you can?"

"Maybe."

"You gonna get married again?"

"I don't know."

"They got divorced five years ago," Katie said.

"Your parents," Jesse said.

"Yes," Katie said. "I don't care."

Jesse nodded.

"And I don't want you giving me a lot of crap about broken homes and that shit," Katie said.

"Okay," Jesse said.

"I always been kind of wild," she said.

"Must worry the hell out of your mother," Jesse said.

"She's scared out of her gourd I'll get pregnant, like she did."

"Which was why she married your father?"

"Yeah, and had me."

"Your father worry about you?" Jesse said.

"He's in Louisville, Kentucky," she said.

"So you don't see him so often."

"For sure," she made it one word. "He got married again. Got a kid."

"And," Jesse said, "I gather your mother dates."

183

"She's boy crazy," Katie said. "Like me."

"Or occasionally," Jesse said, "man crazy."

"You mean Harrison? Yeah. I really showed him something. He said he couldn't believe how great I was. He's got this huge yacht and tons of money. My mother's probably jealous. She's always pigging these losers."

"So how'd you meet Harrison?" Jesse said.

"Actually I met Tommy first and he introduced me to Harrison."

"Tommy?" Jesse said.

"Tommy Ralston. He's got a yacht, too. The *Sea Cloud*."

"How'd you meet Tommy?" Jesse said.

"Cathleen Holton," Katie said. "Cathleen brought a bunch of us out to Tommy's boat. She said it was a chance to meet some really cool guys."

"She have a boat?" Jesse said.

"Naw, Tommy sent a launch for us."

"How many were you?"

"Excuse me?"

"How many of you went out."

"Me," she said. "And Cathleen, Beth, Nancy and Brittany, five all together."

"All around your age?"

"I'm the youngest," she said. "I always

hang around with older kids."

Jesse nodded.

"Tell me about what happened on the boat."

"It was wild," Katie said. "There were four guys and a couple of older women. We had drinks, and we smoked some weed, and the guys said it was like an initiation. We all had to have sex with all the guys."

"Everybody cool with that?" Jesse said.

"Everybody but Nancy. She started to cry and said she didn't feel good and wanted to go home."

"And did she?"

"They said they'd have somebody take her home in the launch, but she had to do a striptease first."

"She mind?"

"She didn't want to, but they said she had to if she wanted to go home . . . so she did. It was pretty pathetic."

"And then she went home?"

"Yeah, one of the sailors took her in the launch."

"And the rest of you partied."

"Yes."

"And the older women?"

"First they watched, then they joined in."

"Hell of a good time," Jesse said.

"Sure, and then Tommy said I was so good that he wanted me to meet his dear friend, and said could I come back tomorrow, and I said sure, and so the next day the launch took me to Harrison's boat. Just me."

Jesse was silent. Katie looked at him oddly, like she wanted something. *Jesus Christ, she wants approval.* He took a breath.

"Most people," he said, "are probably doing mostly what they need to do. And maybe you need to do this. But it's not a good way for you to live."

"Why not," she said.

"Again," Jesse said, "long answer. Short version is you don't become more important because a lot of people are willing to fuck you."

"I'm not trying to be important," she said. "I'm just having some fun."

"I need the names of the other girls," Jesse said.

"Are you going to tell them I told?"

Jesse looked at Molly, who had said not a word during the entire conversation. She shrugged and shook her head.

"To tell you the truth, Katie," Jesse said, "I don't know what I'm going to do. But I'll start by taking names."

35

Jenn always brushed her teeth before bed. Jesse lay in bed on his back with his hands clasped behind his head, watching her through the open door of the bathroom. She was wearing one of his shirts, just the way she used to, and when she bent over to rinse her mouth, her butt showed. Jenn turned off the bathroom light and got into bed beside Jesse.

"Were you leering at me?" Jenn said.

"I was admiring your butt," Jesse said.

"It is cute, isn't it."

"So you don't mind admiring," Jesse said.

"Admiring is good; leering is good."

"I was admiring," Jesse said.

Jenn tuned her head and kissed him lightly.

"Tell me about your day," she said.

He knew she was mocking their domesticity.

"Any day that ends up with us in bed," Jesse said, "is a good day."

"Oh," she said, "you charming devil."

"I would like to get through with this floater case," Jesse said. "It's turned into a goddamned cesspool."

"The one where you were watching the dirty movies?"

"Yeah."

"It's gotten worse."

"Want to tell me about it?"

"I do," Jesse said. "It's one of the things I really missed when you were gone."

"Talking to me?"

"I could always talk to you," Jesse said.

"So talk," Jenn said.

They had left the balcony doors open, and they could hear the sound of the harbor as Jesse talked, lying on his back in the nearly dark room, looking up the blank, uninteresting ceiling. Jenn turned on her side toward him as she listened. Through the open French doors, they could hear a boat motor. Softer, more persistent, so familiar in its endless rhythm as to be nearly soundless was the movement of the waves against the causeway at the south end of the harbor. Jenn already knew some of the story, about the videotapes from Darnell. He told her the rest. He told her what Kelly Cruz had learned. He told her about Katie DeWolfe.

"So the bastards recruit?" Jenn said

when he was finished.

"And apparently swap."

"Tapes, too," Jenn said, "wouldn't you guess?"

"They probably leer at them," Jesse said.

"Almost certainly," Jenn said. "And, my God, what about the women on board? You know the older women? What are they?"

"Put the young ones at ease. Maybe. On the other hand, Katie says, they 'jump right in.'"

"Jesus," Jenn said. "You can get them both, can't you? For statutory rape?"

"I can always do that," Jesse said. "I want them for murder."

"Both of them?"

"Whoever killed her," Jesse said. "And whoever helped. And whoever knew."

"What if neither of them did it?" Jenn said.

"One of them did it. Maybe both."

"You're so sure?"

"I'm so sure."

She continued to lie on her side, looking at him. He continued to look at the ceiling.

"If I was looking at your butt and just thinking it was a good-looking butt?" Jesse said after a while.

"That would be admiring," Jenn said.

"And if I also imagined holding on to your butt while we were making wild and exotic love?"

"That would be leering."

"And is one better than the other?" Jesse said.

"Jesse, this sex case is making you crazy," Jenn said.

"You think?"

Jenn took in a deep breath.

"I am your main fucking squeeze," she said. "You are supposed to admire me and leer at me and feel desire and act on it."

"Act on it?"

"Yeah, act. That too much for you, Hamlet?"

Jesse grinned at her.

"Then out swords," he said, "and to work withal."

"That's not Hamlet," Jenn said.

"Jose Ferrer said it in some movie I saw."

"That was Cyrano de Bergerac."

"Close enough," Jesse said, and pressed his mouth on hers.

36

"Thanks for coming in, Mr. Ralston," Jesse said.

Thomas Ralston's head was shaved. He had a deep tan. He was a little taller than Jesse. Six feet, maybe. And he was the kind of fat guy who pretends that it's brawn. His white shirt had epaulets. It was unbuttoned halfway down his fat tan chest. He had on tan linen slacks and brown leather sandals. A gold cross on a thick chain nestled among the gray chest hairs. He kept his wraparound sunglasses on indoors.

"What's this all about, Chief?" he said.

"Just routine," Jesse said. "We're looking into a homicide. Woman from Fort Lauderdale named Florence Horvath."

"Never heard of her," Ralston said.

"Well, that answers one question," Jesse said. "We think she may have come off one of the yachts here for Race Week."

Ralston shrugged.

"So, you being registered in Fort Lauderdale and all."

"Sure," Ralston said. "Perfectly understandable. Why do you think she fell off a yacht."

"I didn't say she fell," Jesse said.

"Whatever. You got any evidence?"

Jesse took out his head shots from the Horvath video.

"Know any of these three people?" Jesse said.

Ralston studied the pictures for a time, then shook his head and handed them back.

"Don't know any of them," he said.

Ralston took a leather cigar case out of his shirt pocket.

"Care for a cigar, Chief?" Ralston said. "The real thing. I'd deny it in court, of course. But genuine Cuban."

"No thank you," Jesse said.

Ralston shrugged and began to take out a cigar.

"There's a town ordinance against smoking on town property," Jesse said.

Ralston paused and shook his head and then put the cigar back in the case and the case back in his pocket.

"Amazing," he said.

"Know anyone named Katie DeWolfe?" Jessie said.

Jesse could almost hear something click shut inside Ralston. He seemed to think about the name for a moment. Then he shook his head.

"No," he said. "I don't. Why do you ask?"

"Know Harrison Darnell?"

"Darnell?" Ralston said. "Yeah. Sure. I know him a little. Not well. Just casual, you know? Yachting isn't that big a world. He's on the *Lady Jane*, I believe."

"Also out of Fort Lauderdale," Jesse said.

"Oh, sure, that's right. Of course. That's why you're asking. The Fort Lauderdale connection."

"You think he might know Florence Horvath?" Jesse said.

"I just have no way to know, Chief . . . ?" Ralston looked at the nameplate on Jesse's desk. "Jesse Stone, is it?"

Jesse nodded.

"I don't know who Harrison Darnell knows or what he does."

"What might he do?" Jesse said.

"I just told you I don't know," Ralston said. "I'm trying to be cooperative, Chief, but you seem hostile."

Jesse nodded.

"Know anyone named Cathleen Holton?" Jesse said.

"No."

"How about Corliss or Claudia Plum?"

"No. Who the hell are these people?"

"Mandy Morello?" Jesse said.

"No, for crissake, Chief. What's going on here? You think I did something?"

"No," Jesse said. "Just running through the list."

"Well, no offense, but I'm getting tired of it. Can I leave?"

"Sure," Jesse said. "Thanks for coming in."

37

Kelly Cruz was in the manager's office at the marina near the Boat Club. The manager was appropriately windblown and suntanned, wearing a marina staff polo shirt and khaki shorts. There was, Kelly Cruz noticed, a cute tattoo on his left calf. Kelly Cruz liked tattoos in discreet moderation.

"Wow," the manager said. "You're pretty good-looking, for a cop."

"I'm pretty good-looking for a person," Kelly Cruz said. "My name's Kelly Cruz."

"Bob," the manager said.

"Do you have assigned mooring here, Bob?"

"Sure," the manager said. "Otherwise it'd be a free-for-all when they came in."

"So you got a record of the mooring locations," Kelly Cruz said.

"Course."

The manager had thick black hair, cut short. His forearms and hands looked strong. He was wearing a nice aftershave.

"May I see them?"

"You bet," the manager said. "Come

around, we got it all on computer."

Kelly Cruz stood beside him while he punched up the listings.

"Lookin' for anybody special?" he said.

"Thomas Ralston."

The manager scrolled down.

"Here we go, he owns *Sea Cloud.* Number 10A."

"How about Harrison Darnell?"

The manager scrolled again.

"He should be 8A or 12A. I remember . . . yeah, 12A . . . I remember they made a point of insisting on side-by-side moorings."

"They registered together?"

"We don't call it registered, Kelly. But yeah. They came in a year, year and a half ago, said they wanted to be far out, and they had to be side by side."

"Do you know either of these gentlemen, Bob?"

"Nope. Just saw them when they contracted the moorings."

"Do you know why they wanted to be side by side?"

"Nope."

"A guess?"

"Party together, I suppose. Two boats are better than one?"

"Two of most things are better than one," Kelly Cruz said.

"Absolutely, Detective Kelly Cruz."

"Kelly's my first name."

Bob grinned at her.

"I figured you weren't Irish," he said.

She smiled.

"You know anything interesting about either of these guys?" she said.

"Not a thing."

"Know anybody named Florence Horvath?"

"Nope."

"Corliss or Claudia Plum?"

"Nope. Great names, though," Bob said. "You ever go out with people you've questioned, Kelly Cruz?"

"When I can get a babysitter."

"Kids."

"Yep."

"Husband?"

"Nope."

"That works," Bob said.

"It does," Kelly Cruz said, and handed Bob her card.

38

Healy took his hat off and put it on the edge of Jesse's desk.

"I'm on my way home," he said.

"Way to go," Jesse said.

"Which means I'm off duty."

"Oh, yeah," Jesse said.

He went to the file cabinet, got a bottle of Bushmill's Black Label, poured about two inches into a water glass and handed it to Healy.

"You still can't join me," Healy said.

"Almost eleven months now," Jesse said. "Not yet. Maybe never."

"Day at a time," Healy said.

He took a sip, and put his head back, and closed his eyes.

"You don't have to enjoy it so fucking much," Jesse said.

"Sorry," Healy said. "But you remember what the first one was like at the end of the day."

"I do," Jesse said. "It's the fifth or sixth one I have trouble recalling."

"I'll try to be unemotional about the

next swallow," Healy said.

"Appreciate it."

"So," Healy said. "You asked me to stop by."

"Remember the floater we had?" Jesse said.

"Horvath," Healy said. "Been a long time in the water."

"Well, lemme bring you up to date," Jesse said.

Healy nodded and sat back with his Irish whiskey and listened.

When Jesse was through, Healy thought about things for a moment. Then he said, "You can get them on statutory rape anytime you want."

"Yes."

"But when you do," Healy said, "they'll get lawyered to the eyeballs, and you won't get another word out of them."

"Correct."

"And it's pretty hard to leverage statutory rape into a murder confession."

"Pretty hard," Jesse said.

"So right now you're just stirring the mix."

Jesse nodded.

"So what do you want with me?"

"I don't want to lose them."

"You afraid they'll run?"

"They know I'm interested," Jesse said. "They've got money. They leave the jurisdiction, I'm going to have trouble getting them back."

"Maybe you shouldn't have let them know you were interested."

"Maybe. But I got no other way to go about this than to keep prying and asking and pushing and poking and looking around. And maybe the pressure will make one of them stupid."

Healy nodded. "They aren't charged with a crime," he said. "They can go where they want to."

"But they could be charged with statutory rape anytime," Jesse said.

"So you want me to help you keep track of them and if they try to depart we arrest them and charge them with the rape of a minor child."

"Yes."

"And tell them they have the right to an attorney."

"Better than losing them," Jesse said. "I don't have the resources."

"We can help you at the airport," Healy said. "And the train stations."

"And I need some clout with the Coast Guard. They're stretched a little thin these days."

"I can probably do something there. If I can't, I can probably get you one of ours. What do you want, a patrol boat at the harbor mouth?"

"Plainly marked," Jesse said.

"Soon?"

"Now," Jesse said.

Healy sipped some whiskey.

"Soon," he said.

They sat quietly.

"You got a theory?" Healy said after a time.

"Some kind of sex ring with these two clucks at the center," Jesse said. "They bring some girls and recruit others, mostly very young. Florence would have been a bring-along."

"And you figure something grew out of that scene that caused the death of Horvath?"

"Yes."

"You figure Darnell did it?"

"Yes."

"So where's Ralston fit?"

"I don't know. Maybe nowhere. Maybe he's just a pervert and all we get him on is the stat rape charge."

"Could have been Ralston," Healy said.

"Could have. They were tight, we know that. Cruz in Fort Lauderdale found that out. Moorings at the outer ring. Side by side."

"They were doing the same thing there," Healy said.

"I'd guess," Jesse said.

"You got anywhere to go now?"

"Nothing beyond the rape charge. Hell, I don't even know if that will stick on Ralston. We got Darnell cold with it on tape. But the girl may not be a good witness against Ralston, and we got no tape."

"Keep pushing," Healy said. "These aren't stand-up guys, I'd guess."

"You'd be right," Jesse said.

"And they've made a lot of messes in various places they've been. So one of them will scare and fuck up and you'll catch him and it'll either be him or he'll give you the other one . . ."

"Or one of the messes they left behind will give them up."

Healy nodded. They were quiet again. It was a late summer day. Still light, but the light slanting now from the west, and a darker tone. Healy sipped his whiskey. *It would be nice,* Jesse thought, *to be able to sit at the edge of evening and sip a whiskey and talk. Maybe someday. Maybe not.*

"You're living with your ex-wife," Healy said.

"We're giving it another try."

"Working?"

"So far," Jesse said.

"Good," Healy said, and sipped.

"You're married," Jesse said.

"Long time," Healy said. "Some of it has been some pretty bad thrashing around, but we hung in there and it turned out good."

Jesse nodded.

"Marriage is hard for cops," Healy said. "Know a lot of them that can't do it."

"Cop wasn't the issue, I don't think," Jesse said.

"Some of the divorces are a mess. They hate each other, they fight over the kids and the money and anything else they can find."

"I know marriages like that," Jesse said.

"Yeah. But some of the breakups are bad. They loved each other, even liked each other, but they couldn't do it."

"Hard," Jesse said.

"Hardest thing in the world, I think. Guys like us," Healy said, "are not chit-chat guys. Closed in a little, maybe."

Healy sipped whiskey, and sat a minute as it settled in.

"And the only people we know how to talk with is the women we marry," he said.

"I know," Jesse said.

"Then the marriage breaks up, and you need somebody to talk with more than you ever have and she's the only one you can't talk with. . . . Makes for a lot of guys alone with a bottle of vodka."

"That's why they have shrinks," Jesse said.

"Lot of cops don't do shrinks."

"I do," Jesse said.

"Which is maybe," Healy said, "why she's back in the house."

39

Jenn's dressing room was in the back part of a trailer, the remainder of which served as a production office.

"Just like a movie star," Jesse said.

He sat on the little built-in banquette while Jenn took off her camera makeup.

"Big production budget," Jenn said. "This isn't just Channel Three. This is Allied Broadcasting, which owns five other stations in big markets all across the country. New York, Chicago, L.A. This is like national."

Jenn washed her face carefully in the small bathroom, and came out and dried carefully, and began to reapply her own makeup.

"Why not just leave the other makeup on?" Jesse said.

Jenn glanced at him in the mirror.

"Don't be silly," she said.

"Just asking," Jesse said.

Jenn leaned very close to the mirror as she worked on her face.

"When I get through," she said, "I have

something really interesting to show you. You know what B roll is?"

"Sure, second unit. No stars or anything, just the director and a camera guy getting background stuff."

"Second unit," Jenn said. "I forget you worked all those years in L.A."

"Everybody in L.A. knows second unit," Jesse said. "Hell I can even say mise-en-scène."

"But can you define it?" Jenn said.

"Nope. I left L.A. before I learned that part."

Jenn put her lip gloss on and leaned back a little and looked at herself in the mirror. Then she leaned very close and looked. Then back for one more medium-range look and turned toward him.

"Check this out," Jenn said.

She put a cassette in the built-in VCR and pressed play. It was raw film, taken on board several yachts in Paradise Harbor. Jesse watched silently. There was no dialogue.

"I was looking at some of the B roll," Jenn said. "Marty's great. She wants my input on everything. And I saw something that I thought would interest you."

"You want to say what?"

"You'll see," Jenn said.

Jesse watched silently. The scenes jerked from one to another without transition.

"Yo!" Jesse said.

Jenn stopped the tape and rewound it, and played it again.

"Yo," Jesse said.

"See him?" Jenn said.

"From the Florence Horvath sex tape," Jesse said.

"Part of the fuck sandwich," Jenn said. "The one on top, I think."

"And you recognized him," Jesse said.

"I did."

"You must have been paying closer attention to that tape than I thought," Jesse said.

"I'm naturally observant," Jenn said. "You recognized him, too."

"I'm supposed to," Jesse said. "Was this a test?"

Jenn smiled. "I guess it was. I guess I would have kind of liked it if you'd missed him and I had to point him out."

"Glad I passed," Jesse said.

"Well," Jenn said after a pause, "I guess I am, too."

"Sign of love," Jesse said.

"Yes."

"You know where the tape was made?" Jesse said.

"Everything's labeled," Jenn said. "So when we get in the editing room, we have some idea of what we're doing."

"Clever," Jesse said. "And the location is?"

"*Sea Cloud*," Jenn said. "Yesterday. Contact Thomas Ralston."

"Yesterday," Jesse said.

Jenn nodded.

"We always date everything," Jenn said.

"The sonovabitch is still here," Jesse said.

Jenn shrugged.

"I need a copy of that tape," Jesse said.

"Take it," Jenn said. "I had them dupe it for you."

"Christ," Jesse said. "Maybe you should be chief of police."

"What," Jenn said. "And give up show business?"

40

His name was Eric Jurgen. Suitcase
Simpson and Arthur Angstrom went out to
the *Sea Cloud* and got him.

"Thanks for coming in, Mr. Jurgen,"
Jesse said.

"I try to obey the police," Jurgen answered.

He spoke with a faint accent.

"Are you foreign born, Mr. Jurgen?"
Jesse said.

"I am Austrian," Jurgen said. "Is there a
problem?"

"You are a crewman on the *Sea Cloud*,"
Jesse said.

"Yes sir."

"Do you know Florence Horvath?"

Jurgen smiled. "Florence," he said. "Yes.
I am very sorry to hear that she died."

"How did you know her?"

"She was with Mr. Darnell when I
worked on the *Lady Jane*."

"With Mr. Darnell?"

"You know, like his girlfriend."

"Didn't Mr. Darnell have several girl-
friends?" Jesse said.

Again Jurgen smiled.

"Yes sir," Jurgen said. "Many. But Florence was . . . she was like the head girlfriend."

"I have a copy of a videotape," Jesse said, "which shows you and another man having simultaneous sex with Florence Horvath."

"Oh," Jurgen said. "Oh my. You have that tape."

"I do," Jesse said.

"Have I broken the law?" Jurgen said.

"No," Jesse said. "I'd just like you to tell me a little about the tape, if you would."

"I . . . I do not know what to tell you," Jurgen said. "I have done that never before."

"Had sex for the camera?"

"No, that either," Jurgen said. "But I have never shared a woman. It is very embarrassing."

"Who's the other guy?"

"My brother."

"His name is Jurgen, too?"

"Yes. Konrad."

"How'd the tape come about?"

"Florence wanted to make it."

"Why?"

"I don't know. She was living on the boat. We were crew. Everyone else was ashore."

"Darnell there?"

"God, no. I could not do that in front of another man."

"Except your brother."

"That is different," Jurgen said.

"Where were you moored?"

"Fort Lauderdale."

"Who took the pictures," Jesse said.

"Her sisters."

"Florence Horvath's sisters," Jesse said.

"Yes."

"Corliss and Claudia Plum."

"I think so, I don't really remember the names very well but that sounds as if it is correct."

"And this was Florence's idea."

"The whole thing," Jurgen said.

"She approached my brother and myself," Jurgen said. "We were embarrassed. But we are brothers. I could not do such a thing with a stranger."

"How about the Plum sisters?"

"Oh, yes. We didn't know them. But they were not, ah, actively involved, if you see what I mean. And besides, they were girls. I wouldn't want another man watching."

They were quiet. Jurgen sat obediently, waiting for another question.

"Anyone enjoy this pig pile?" Jesse said.

"Well, it was . . . different," Jurgen said. "If a man crews on this yacht circuit, he gets a lot of sex. It's pretty routine after a while. This was . . ."

He rolled his right hand as he tried to think of the right word.

"It was unusual," he said.

"How about Florence?"

"I guess she liked it," Jurgen said. "She was quite interested in the filming, though."

"And you did this because she asked you."

"Yes. I liked Florence. Kon, my brother, and I both liked her."

"She pay you?"

"No sir, absolutely not, sir. She did not pay us anything."

"No offense," Jesse said. "You have any idea how she died?"

"No sir."

"Where's your brother?"

"In the Caribbean, sir. On Mr. Damon's boat."

"Where's Mr. Damon from?"

"Boat's out of Miami, sir. I don't know if Mr. Damon lives there."

"First name?"

"Mr. Damon? I don't know, sir."

"And where do you live when you're not on a boat?"

"Miami, sir. Kon and I have a condo."

Jesse pushed a pad of paper toward Jurgen.

"Write down the address," Jesse said.

Jurgen did. Jesse took the pad back and looked at it.

"Gimme your driver's license," Jesse said.

Jurgen produced it and Jesse compared addresses. They were the same. Jesse gave the license back and grinned at Jurgen.

"Suspicious by nature," Jesse said.

"That is fine, sir. I know you have a job to do."

Jesse nodded.

"I'd like it if you didn't talk about this conversation."

"They will ask me, sir."

"Tell them it was routine. I simply asked you if you'd observed anything unusual on board."

"My God, sir . . ."

Jesse put up his hand.

"Just say you told me no."

Jurgen smiled.

"If you say so, sir," he said.

41

Jesse had a drink with Rita Fiore at the Seaport Hotel on the South Boston harborfront.

"Thanks for coming out here through the Big fucking Dig," Rita said. "But I've been in federal court most of the day and needed a double martini immediately after."

"Glad to oblige," Jesse said.

"You drinking Coke?"

"Yes."

"On the wagon?"

"Eleven months," Jesse said.

"Eek," Rita said.

She drank some of her martini.

"That's like the last time I saw you," she said.

"I stopped shortly after."

"Scared you sober, huh?"

Jesse smiled.

"There were other issues," he said.

"Yeah. I know. Like the ex-wifey-do."

"She would be one," Jesse said.

"How you and she doing."

Jesse held up crossed fingers.

"We're living together at the moment."

"Oh," Rita said, "how nice for you."

"Aw, come on," Jesse said. "You and I weren't going anywhere."

"Maybe *you* weren't," Rita said.

"You were?"

"Seemed like a good idea at the time," Rita said.

Jesse didn't say anything. Rita wore her thick copper hair long. She was wearing a short skirt, and sitting sideways on the bar stool with her legs crossed. Jesse studied her for a moment. Rita watched him and raised her eyebrows.

"You would be a good idea," Jesse said. "Anytime."

"But not a keeper," Rita said.

Jesse smiled and didn't answer. Rita gestured to the bartender for another martini. She turned back toward Jesse and smiled widely.

"Okay, so you're not here to propose," she said.

"I sent a couple of sisters to you awhile ago," Jesse said.

"The Plum twins," Rita said.

"Anything work out?" Jesse said.

"Hey, you think just because you got my clothes off a couple of times, I'll betray professional confidences?"

"I was hoping," Jesse said.

"Actually they didn't employ me. I have no obligations to them. They wanted help finding out who killed their sister."

Jesse nodded.

"I sent them to a guy I know. But it didn't work out."

"They see him at all?"

"Yes," Rita said. "But they didn't tell him anything and when he asked them stuff they were evasive, so he told them to blow."

"Excuse me?" Jesse said.

"In a manner of speaking," Rita said.

"They say anything to you?" Jesse said.

"I think they were worried that you are a small-town doofus," Rita said, "rather than a high-powered urban hotshot . . . like, say, me."

"Anything else?"

"I'd say their combined intelligence is about that of a mud puddle."

Jesse nodded.

"They told me they were staying at the Four Seasons," he said.

"Yep. That's what they told me."

"Too bad they didn't hook up with your guy."

Rita shook her head.

"He wouldn't have told you anything. He's a very hard case."

"Just right for you," Jesse said.

Rita shook her head slowly.

"Fat chance," she said. "He's in love with a shrink."

"Probably handy to have one in house," Jesse said.

"Certainly would cut down on the travel time," Rita said. "What's your interest in the Plum girls?"

"They might be a little less innocent in all this than they claim."

"But no smarter."

"God, no," Jesse said.

"Tell me," Rita said.

Jesse drank some of his Coke.

"All of it?" he said.

"Keep you talking," Rita said, "you may weaken."

"Especially if you ply me with Coca-Cola," Jesse said.

"Have another," Rita said.

They both smiled. And Jesse told her what he knew about the death of Florence Horvath. When Rita listened, Jesse noticed, the sexual challenge left her face.

"Wow," she said when Jesse was through.

"Yeah," Jesse said.

"I've been a prosecutor," Rita said, "and

a defense attorney. I've been on one side or another of criminal law all my adult life."

Jesse nodded.

"I have also probably slept with more men than you've arrested."

"And I'm a good cop," Jesse said.

"And I'm shocked."

"Yeah," Jesse said. "It's pretty bad."

"It's disgusting," Rita said.

"But only some of it is illegal," Jesse said.

"Enough of it," Rita said. "These aren't people society has abandoned. They didn't grow up with no parents in some goddamned project someplace. They're not victims of racism, or class contempt or poverty. They have no excuse for being trash."

"True," Jesse said.

"This is bothering the hell out of me," Rita said. "And I'm not even involved."

"I know," Jesse said.

"Doesn't it bother you? The obsession with sex, devoid of affection? The exploitation of young girls? The . . ." Rita waved her hands. "The lack of any feeling anywhere among any of these fucking automatons?"

"I have my own problems with it," Jesse said. "But I try not to let it interfere with the work."

Rita sat back a little on the bar stool and looked at Jesse and nodded slowly.

"And," she said, "you haven't had two martinis on an empty stomach."

"Sadly, no," Jesse said.

42

Jesse sat with the Plum twins on a bench in the Public Garden, across from the hotel, near the Swan Boats.

"Our room is such a mess," Corliss said.

"The maid hasn't cleaned up yet," Claudia said.

"This is fine," Jesse said. "Right here."

"What would be a trip," Corliss said, "would be to get high and take a ride on those boats."

"At night," Claudia said.

"You took the pictures of your sister and the two men," Jesse said.

"Whaa?" Corliss said.

"You took the threesome video of your sister."

"We did not," Claudia said.

"Not," Corliss said.

"Yeah," Jesse said. "Eric already told me, and Kon will say so as well."

"How do you know Eric?" Corliss said.

"I'm the chief of police," Jesse said. "I know everything."

"You know Konrad?" Claudia said.

Jesse smiled.

"So what's up with that?" he said.

Both of them giggled. Jesse wasn't sure at what. Maybe that was a Plum family technique. When in doubt, giggle. He waited. They looked at each other.

"Flo," Corliss said. "Flo asked us to."

"On Darnell's boat," Jesse said.

"Ohh, you know that," Claudia said.

Jesse nodded. No one said anything. Full of adults and children, the Swan Boats elegantly pedaled their slow circuit of the pond.

"Flo wanted us to do it that way," Corliss said.

They seemed to speak with instinctive deference to each other's turn.

"Why?" Jesse said.

Again the girls looked at each other. "She wanted to jerk Harry's chain," Claudia said.

"Harry?"

"Harrison," Corliss said.

"Darnell," Jesse said.

Both girls nodded.

"Because?"

"Because he dumped her," Claudia said.

"She was his girlfriend?" Jesse said.

Both girls laughed.

"Aren't you funny," Corliss said.

"What was their relationship?" Jesse said.

"She was the one, you know," Claudia said, "the one he kept."

"And the other women?"

"Entertainment, you know?" Corliss said.

"Like fishing," Claudia said, "or skeet, or bridge."

"And Florence didn't mind them?"

"Not as long as she had her place," Corliss said.

"Which was?" Jesse said.

"Head nigger," Claudia said.

Both girls giggled again.

"But Darnell reorganized?" Jesse said.

"He dumped her," Corliss said. "For Blondie Martin."

"And Florence took this video on his boat to make him jealous?" Jesse said.

"She would never do it with him," Claudia said.

"Harrison was always after her to go with him and Tommy Ralston," Corliss said.

"But she wouldn't."

"No. But when he dumped her . . ."

"She done it with a couple of former crew guys, and sent him the tape."

"To make him jealous."

"Yeah."

"Did it work?"

"He sent for her," Corliss said. "Flew her up to Boston."

"There's no record of her flying to Boston," Jesse said.

"He had his pilot fly her up in his private plane."

"When?"

"Beginning of June," Corliss said.

"She told us he was up here early for Race Week and she was going to join him."

"What is the pilot's name?" Jesse said.

The sisters looked at each other. They both shrugged.

"Larry," Corliss said.

"Last name?"

They both shook their heads.

"Just Larry is all we ever knew," Claudia said.

They watched the Swan Boats for a time. Some squirrels darted among the attendant pigeons, hoping for a peanut.

"So how come you didn't tell me any of this before?" Jesse said.

Both sisters shrugged.

"I guess we thought you'd be mad," Corliss said.

"Mad?"

"You know, about us sneaking on the boat and taking the pictures. We were afraid you'd say something to Willis and

Betsy," Claudia said.

"Your parents?"

"Yes."

"Why do you care?" Jesse said.

"They still got some control of our trust funds."

"Of course," Jesse said. "So why'd you come up here and see me?"

"We liked Flo. We felt bad about her."

"And you wanted to know what I knew," Jesse said. "For fear it might come out."

"If someone hurt Flo," Claudia said, "we wanted to know. We wanted to help."

"So you set up headquarters here," Jesse said, glancing behind him at the hotel, "and began to ferret out the truth."

"We're having a pretty good time here," Corliss said. "You ever do two guys and a woman?"

"No."

"We like two women and a guy," Claudia said, and pressed her breast against Jesse's left shoulder.

It had no part in the investigation. The question wasn't professional. But Jesse couldn't help it.

"Ever think about love?" Jesse said.

The twins stared at him for a time and then giggled.

43

Leaning their backsides against the trunk of her car, Kelly Cruz and Larry Barnes stood and talked and watched the private planes land and take off from Fort Lauderdale Executive Airport.

"You flew Florence Horvath up to Boston," Kelly Cruz said, "in June."

"Yeah, sure, I remember, last month."

"That would be June," Kelly Cruz said.

Barnes grinned at her. He had a thick black mustache and longish hair and big aviator glasses and a short-sleeved white shirt. And his big silver wristwatch looked complex. Neatly across his right forearm just above the wrist was a tattoo that read BAD NEWS.

"Tell me about the trip," Kelly Cruz said.

"Mr. Darnell called, said he wanted me to bring her up. Told me she'd be in touch to arrange the schedule."

"Darnell often do this?"

Barnes's face didn't change, but somehow Kelly Cruz knew he was amused.

"Often," he said.

"With different women?"

"Often," Barnes said.

"Anything unusual about this flight?"

"She required Cristal on ice instead of Krug."

"What was Florence Horvath like?" Kelly Cruz said.

Barnes looked at her and she knew he was even more amused.

"How much of this is on the record," Barnes said.

"Only the questions of fact. Did you take her? When? At whose request? Your opinions are between me and you."

Barnes nodded.

"She was like about two hundred other bimbettes I've transported," Barnes said. "Blond, stupid, sure she was sexy. Asked me if I had ever done it at thirty thousand feet."

Kelly Cruz nodded.

"And you left her in Boston," she said.

"Private terminal. Carried her bags in for her. She was pretty well fried. Gave her to the limo driver. Got the plane serviced, refueled, came on home."

"Happen to know what limo company?"

Barnes shook his head.

"Nope. Just a limo guy with a sign," he said.

"And you never went back to get her," Kelly Cruz said.

"No. I usually didn't. Most of the babes were one-way. I'd fly them someplace and Mr. Darnell would sail them home."

"Know anybody named Thomas Ralston?"

"Fat guy, thinks he looks better than he does?"

"I don't know," Kelly Cruz said. "I've never seen him. I'm helping out some police up north."

"What is this all about, anyway?" Barnes said.

Kelly Cruz smiled.

"So you know Thomas Ralston?"

"Yeah, sure, I think so. Mr. Ralston. He flies a lot with Mr. Darnell."

"Where?"

"Ports usually. Crew sails the boat somewhere and Darnell meets them there. I guess Ralston has the same deal. I never asked."

"Did you fly either of them up to Boston?" Kelly Cruz said.

"Not this year."

"Anyone fly with them?"

"Usual bevy of beauties," Barnes said. "They get drunk. Do some dope."

"Sex?"

He shrugged and gestured.

"I stay up front," he said. "But yeah, I'd say quite a lot."

"And you know this how?"

Barnes looked at her for a moment with the expressionless hint of humor that he projected.

"Ah, trace evidence," he said.

"Thank you," Kelly Cruz said, and closed her notebook.

"What'd they do up north?" Barnes said.

Kelly Cruz took a card out of her purse, and gave it to him.

"Florence Horvath died up there under unusual circumstances," she said. "You think of anything interesting, call me."

Barnes took the card.

"They think Darnell killed her?"

"I don't know what their theory of the case is," Kelly Cruz said. "I'm just asking questions for them."

"Actually, I'm thinking of something sort of interesting right now," he said.

"Not at thirty thousand feet," Kelly Cruz said.

" 'Course not," Barnes said. "Who's going to fly the plane?"

44

Jesse and Molly sat at the conference table in the squad room. The sound of shouting and loud bad singing came from the four-cell jail wing.

"Hark," Jesse said.

"Drunk and disorderly," Molly said. "On Front Street."

"Today?"

"Un-huh."

Jesse looked at his watch.

"It's ten in the morning," he said.

"No time to waste," Molly said.

Jesse nodded. Molly had a big yellow legal-sized pad of blue-lined paper in front of her.

"Okay," he said. "Here's what we've got. We know Florence Horvath was alive when she came up here first week in June. We can probably pin that down exactly if we need to."

Molly made a note. Jesse stood and walked the length of the squad room and looked out the back window at the Public Works garage behind the station.

"And we know she was dead when she washed ashore the beginning of Race Week."

"July twelfth," Molly said.

"ME says she's been in the water at least a couple weeks, maybe longer," Jesse said. "She was alive when she went in the water, but exact cause of death is uncertain due to the ratty condition of the body."

"You have to say *ratty?*"

Jesse turned and walked back the length of the room.

"We know she came up here at Darnell's request, and on his dime. We know she knew Thomas Ralston. We know Ralston and Darnell are connected and a lot tighter than either would admit. Everybody has lied about who they know. We know that Florence made the sex video with the two guys who used to work on Darnell's boat. We know her twin sisters took the video. They said she told them that it was to make Darnell jealous because he had dumped her in favor of Blondie Martin. We know, because we checked the harbor registry, that both Darnell's boat and Ralston's boat were here in early June."

Jesse turned and walked back toward the window.

"So where's the video," Molly said.

Jesse stopped.

"The video?"

"She must have sent it to him," Molly said. "What happened to it?"

"Destroyed it," Jesse said. "It was incriminating to have, and he didn't know there were other copies. We know that there's some kind of high-tech sex thing going on between Ralston and Darnell. And we know they have recruited local, and very young, talent."

"This is probably not the only place," Molly said.

"Probably not. We'll see if Healy can help us with that."

Jesse continued to look at the Public Works garage. Along one side of the garage, snowplow blades were lined up, waiting for winter. They looked like the skeletal remains of extinct beasts in the hot summer sun.

"We know both Darnell and Ralston have committed statutory rape," he said. "And we're pretty sure we can convict them. Darnell for sure. We've got him on tape. Ralston too if the kid will hold up in court."

"And none of this tells us if either or both of them murdered Florence

Horvath," Molly said.

"Sad but true," Jesse said.

He turned and began the trip back up the room toward Molly.

"In fact," Molly said, "we can't really prove that she was murdered at all."

"She was murdered and Darnell was involved," Jesse said.

"How about Ralston?"

"Yes," Jesse said.

"Him, too?"

"Yes."

"You're so sure," Molly said.

"I know them," Jesse said. "I understand them. Darnell and Ralston killed her."

"Together?"

"Don't know."

"But you know they did."

"Yes," Jesse said.

He was standing beside Molly. She looked up at him.

"Intuition?" she said.

"I've been a cop for a long time," Jesse said.

"There's something else," Molly said.

She had turned in her chair and was facing Jesse, looking up at him as he stood in front of her.

"Maybe I'm a little bit like them," Jesse said.

"The hell you are," Molly said.

Jesse shrugged.

"I mean it," Molly said. "You are in no way like either of those two scumbags."

"Scumbags?" Jesse said. "Strong language for a Catholic girl."

"Scumbags," Molly said, "all of them. The men, the women, the damned victim. All of them. After I just talk about them, for God's sake, I feel like I should take a long shower."

"We do know more about them than anyone would want," Jesse said. "That's how murder investigations sometimes go. You accumulate evidence and accumulate evidence and a lot of it makes you want to puke and most of it doesn't solve your case."

"So how are you going to solve this one?"

"Same old way," Jesse said. "Keep asking. Keep pushing. Try to scare them. Maybe somebody will roll on somebody. Maybe somebody will do something stupid."

"Little hard to get somebody to roll on a murder rap by threatening them with stat rape," Molly said.

"You might if you were willing to let one of them walk," Jesse said.

"Are you?"

"No," Jesse said.

"Accomplice testimony doesn't get you

anything in court, anyway," Molly said.

Jesse sat on the edge of the conference table near Molly.

"Doesn't matter," Jesse said. "I'm going to get them both."

They were quiet. Molly doodled a frowning happy face on her yellow pad. Jesse sat on the table edge and let his feet swing.

"You and Jenn okay?" Molly said.

"Yes."

"Living together is okay?"

"Yes."

"So far."

"God, you're cautious about this," Molly said.

"I worry that I'll do it again," Jesse said.

"Do what?"

"Whatever drove her away last time."

"Maybe she did something," Molly said.

"I mean I know she did things, cheated on me and stuff, but what did I do to cause it."

"Maybe nothing," Molly said. "Maybe it was her fault."

Jesse shook his head.

"Course," Molly said. "If it's her fault you got no control over it. Your fault, you do. You can be very careful."

Jesse continued to look out the window.

After a time he said, "Thanks, Molly."

And Molly left.

45

"When I'm stuck," Healy said, "I go over it."

"All of it," Jesse said.

"Start at page one of my notebook and go page by page all the way through."

It was Sunday. They were on his balcony looking at the harbor. Healy had a can of beer. Jesse was drinking Coke. Jenn was in the production office looking at videotape. On the floor of the patio a thick-bodied, middle-aged Welsh corgi lay on his side, his eyes closed, his nose pointed at the ocean. Jesse had put a soup bowl full of water near him. The soup bowl was white with a blue line around the rim.

"I know," Jesse said.

"But you don't want to," Healy said.

"I don't."

"I'll do it with you," Healy said. "A second set of ears."

"On a Sunday?"

"Sure."

"It'll take all day."

"Not a problem," Healy said.

"Something bad going on at your house?" Jesse said.

"My wife's younger brother is visiting with his wife," Healy said. "They have young children."

"You don't care for young children."

"Neither one of us," Healy said. "But it's her brother."

"And the dog?"

"They annoy the hell out of Buck," Healy said. "When he can, he bites them."

"So it wasn't all about helping me when you dropped by."

"It was nothing about that," Healy said. "Why don't you get your notebook."

Jesse went to his bedroom and got the notebook and brought it back.

"You want another beer?" he said.

"No," Healy said. "I'm fine."

Jesse always marveled at people who could nurse any drink. He had already finished his Coke.

"Okay," he said. "She washes ashore near the town wharf. . . ."

And they went through it. Incident by incident. Interview by interview. Day by day.

"Cruz broad sounds pretty good," Healy said at one point.

Jesse nodded.

"People don't always work that hard to clear somebody else's case," Healy said.

"I think she's kind of hooked into it," Jesse said. "Talking to all the people."

Healy nodded.

"Happens," he said.

Jesse went on.

"I went aboard when everyone was at the clambake," he read.

"With a warrant," Healy said.

Jesse smiled, and didn't say anything.

"Okay," Healy said. "No warrant. I, of course, don't know that and never thought to ask."

"Absolutely," Jesse said.

He went on. Healy listened. At one point Buck got up and drank water loudly from the blue-rimmed soup bowl. When he was through he went back to where had been, turned around twice and reassumed his position, with his nose pointed seaward.

"The twins told their parents they were in Europe," Jesse said. "But they were actually in Sag Harbor, New York, with some guy named Carlos Coca."

"You check that?" Healy said.

"No."

"There's a loose end," Healy said.

"Here's another one," Jesse said. "They say they learned of their sister's death from someone named Kimmy Young."

"Haven't checked her out, either," Healy said.

"No."

"Happens," Healy said.

"Shouldn't," Jesse said.

Healy shrugged.

"Where's Kimmy Young from?"

"Don't know," Jesse said. "I assume South Florida."

"I'll bet Kelly Cruz can find her," Healy said.

Jesse nodded. He went back to the notes. It was late afternoon when they finished. Jesse had drunk four Cokes. Healy had nearly finished his beer.

"You don't like to drink?" Jesse said when he picked up the can and found it not quite empty.

"I like to drink," Healy said. "But I only like to drink a small amount."

"Hard to imagine," Jesse said.

"Never liked being drunk," Healy said.

Jesse nodded. Jenn came in through the front door and walked to the balcony. Buck raised his head, looked at her carefully and put his head back down. Jenn saw Healy's beer can. Jesse saw her eyes flick to him. She saw the Coca-Cola can.

"Captain Healy," Jenn said with a big

smile. "How nice to see you."

Jenn was dressed in what she considered weekend leisure wear. Yellow running shoes with pale green laces. Green cargo pants with a studded yellow belt. A yellow top, a choker of green beads around her neck and jade earrings.

"Nice to see you, too," Healy said. "Nice to see you here."

"I know," Jenn said.

Jenn crouched on her heels beside the dog. The movement made the cargo pants very smooth along her thighs and butt. Buck opened his black eyes and made a small movement with his miniscule tail.

"Is that a wag," Jenn said.

"It is."

"What's his name?"

"Buck."

"May I pat him?" she said.

"Sure," Healy said. "He only bites kids."

"Can't blame him for that, can we?"

"Hell no," Healy said. "Bite them myself if I wasn't worried about my pension."

46

Kelly Cruz sat courtside at the Tennis Club with Mrs. Plum while Mr. Plum played men's doubles. Kelly Cruz had an iced tea. Mrs. Plum was drinking gin and tonic.

"Your husband plays very well," Kelly Cruz said.

"Yes," she said. "Doubles."

"Not a good singles player?" Kelly Cruz said.

"No. I don't think he could take the stress of one-to-one confrontation. Inferior players used to beat him regularly. He rarely plays singles anymore."

"He's more of a team player," Kelly Cruz said, to be saying something.

Mrs. Plum didn't comment.

"I'm sorry to bother you again," Kelly Cruz said.

Mrs. Plum drank some gin and tonic. She shrugged.

"It's not like my days are filled with important matters," she said.

Kelly Cruz smiled. She felt very bad for Mrs. Plum.

"Do you know anyone named Kimmy Young?"

"Kimmy Young," Mrs. Plum said, and took another drink. "Kimmy Young. Yes, of course, she was in school with my twins. She used to come over sometimes. Pajama parties. CDs. Brownies. You know how teenagers are. Her mother was Miss Oklahoma when she was a girl. Married Randy Young, Young Financial Services. He's done really wonderfully well."

"Do you know where I might find her?"

"The Youngs moved to Sarasota, I think. They found life in Miami a little fast, I suspect."

Kelly Cruz glanced around at the sea of tennis whites. Mrs. Plum noticed.

"They're somewhat younger than we are," she said. "I suppose we've slowed our pace a bit."

"Did the girls go to private school?"

"Oh yes."

"Which one."

"Vandersea," Mrs. Plum said. "The Vandersea School."

"Here in Miami?"

"Yes."

Kelly Cruz wrote briefly in her notebook. Mrs. Plum flagged down a waiter and got another drink.

241

"Why are you asking about Kimmy?"

"Her name came up in that same case up north," Kelly Cruz said.

"Kimmy was a nice girl," Mrs. Plum said, watching her husband serve. "Smart."

He had a nice hard serve, but Kelly Cruz noticed Mr. Plum didn't follow it in. She didn't know much about tennis; maybe it was strategy.

"Know anyone named Carlos Coca?" Kelly Cruz said as she wrote.

"Heavens, no," Mrs. Plum said.

Kelly Cruz nodded, and kept writing. The Plums probably wouldn't know the Cocas.

"It must be exciting being a, ah, policewoman," Mrs. Plum said.

"Not too much excitement," Kelly Cruz said. "Lots of asking questions and taking notes."

"But it must give you some satisfaction. Solving crimes. That must seem important."

Kelly Cruz put the notebook into her purse beside her gun.

"It does," she said. "Trouble is, then another crime comes along and you're slogging along again."

"This is the most important thing I'll do today," Mrs. Plum said.

Kelly Cruz didn't say anything.

"The money, you know. The money guts you. After a while all you have left to do is look nice, and drink."

Kelly Cruz stood and put her hand out.

"Thank you very much," she said.

Mrs. Plum shook her hand and smiled absently and began to look for the waiter.

47

Jesse was on the phone with Carlos Coca in Sag Harbor.

"Who'd you say you were?" Coca said.

"Jesse Stone. I'm chief of police in Paradise, Massachusetts."

"And why do I want to talk with you?" Coca said.

"So I won't get a couple of big mean New York state troopers to come over and yank you out of your swimming pool," Jesse said.

"I'm not in my pool."

"Figure of speech," Jesse said. "Tell me about Corliss and Claudia Plum."

There was silence. Jesse waited.

"Dumb and dumber," Coca said after awhile. "Yeah, they were here."

"When."

"Early in the summer. Memorial Day weekend, I think. Kinda cool. Not good party weather."

"How long did they stay?"

"Too long," Coca said. "I kicked them out after about three days."

"Why?"

"They didn't fit in," Coca said.

"How so?"

"They're fucking crazy, awright? They were drunk by noon. Walked around topless. I got a lot of top-drawer people here. Christ, I got the president of a real estate development company. Big company. International. He's sitting outside with his wife, having a cocktail before lunch. One of them, who the fuck knows which one, topless, thong bikini bottom, goes and sits in his lap. Takes a drink from his glass. Man!"

"Wasn't she cold?" Jesse said.

"Who, Missy Hot Bottom? I don't know. Why?"

"You said it was cool."

"Well, hell," Coca said. "I'm not even sure what weekend. All my weekends are pretty lively. But I'm pretty sure nobody was swimming."

"So the bikini was for effect."

"Sure, those two assholes don't do anything except for effect. For crissake, some of my important guests left because of them."

"And how do you know them?" Jesse said.

"Their sister."

"Florence?"

"Yeah. Now *there* was a babe. She was even wilder than the twins, but she had a little class. You know? She never offended any of my guests. And she could hold her booze."

"She brought her sisters to party with you?" Jesse said.

"Not this year, they came on their own, but yeah, they used to come with her. Hell, they were still jailbait when they started coming here. The jailbait twins."

"They get along?"

"Sure. It was like Florence was showing them the ropes. Like she was breaking them in."

"Lot of sex at your parties?" Jesse said.

"Hey," Coca said. "What about privacy here. I'm entitled to my privacy."

"I don't care if your guests had carnal knowledge of a vending machine," Jesse said. "I'm only interested in my case. Anything you tell me is off the record."

"Well, sure. There's usually some sex at a big weekend party, you know? Why wouldn't there be? I think it's one reason Flo brought her sisters. Learn their way around, in a safe environment."

"Safe environment?" Jesse said.

"Yeah. There's always a good class of people at my parties. Good place for young

246

girls to, you know, grow up."

"Even when they were jailbait?" Jesse said.

"Not with me," Coca said. "But yeah. There's guys like them young. It wasn't like anyone's first time."

"Any idea where anyone might have lost her cherry?"

"Got me," Coca said. "Flo told me they weren't virgins."

"Know where they were headed when you gave them the boot?" Jesse said.

"Nope. They packed up, and my driver took them into the city and dropped them."

"Where?"

"He said he took them to the Peninsula Hotel."

"And this would have been the beginning of June?"

"Yeah, sure, first week or so for sure."

"And you haven't heard from them since?"

"No. What's this all about, anyway? What'd they do?"

"Just routine stuff, Mr. Coca, names came up in a case here."

"Flo involved?"

"Indirectly," Jesse said.

"Well, Flo had more class, but they're all

crazy. Whole goddamned family was crazy, Flo said."

"Whole family?"

"Yeah. That's what she used to say."

"Any details?"

"No, just that they were all crazy. That the money had ruined them all."

"You think she was including her parents?" Jesse said.

"She never said. All of them seemed kind of hung up on the old man."

"How so?" Jesse said.

"What am I, fucking Dr. Phil? They just talked about him a lot. Daddy this, Daddy that. Like he mattered."

"Parents do," Jesse said.

"Yeah. I've heard that."

"Can you think of anything they said about Daddy?"

"You listen to those fucking twins for long, your brain fries," Coca said. "You know what I'm saying? I worked my fucking ass off not to pay any attention to them. Mostly they fucking giggle."

"So you can't remember an example."

"What'd I just say, for crissake."

"That you can't remember an example," Jesse said. "Thanks for your time, Mr. Coca. I may call back in a few days, see if anything has occurred to you."

"I hope not," Coca said.

After he had hung up the phone Jesse sat in his office and swiveled his chair aimlessly. Then he swiveled back and picked up the phone and called Kelly Cruz.

48

Kelly Cruz sat in the small living room of Kimmy Young's apartment in Coconut Grove.

"How'd you find me?" Kimmy said.

"Vandersea alumnae office," Kelly Cruz said.

"God," Kimmy said. "They never lose you, do they? CIA ought to use them."

Kelly Cruz smiled.

"Let me tell you why I'm here," she said.

"Yes ma'am," Kimmy said.

"My name is Kelly Cruz, I hope you'll call me Kelly."

"I'm Kimmy."

"Okay," Kelly Cruz said. "We have that settled."

Kimmy was blond, of course. *Everyone is blond, except Detective Cruz.* She was pretty but overweight, and she had a cheerful manner.

"You know Corliss and Claudia Plum," Kelly Cruz said.

"I went to school with them."

"And did you inform them of their sister's death?"

"Flo?"

"Florence Horvath."

"She's dead?" Kimmy said.

"She is."

"My God!" Kimmy said.

"I'm guessing that you didn't inform them of Florence's death."

"God, no."

"So how did they hear of it?"

"I don't know. I haven't seen them in years."

"Really?"

"Years. Not since I was, like, fifteen."

"And you are?"

"I'll be twenty-one in August."

"And are you in school?"

"I'm going into my senior year at U. Miami."

"Your family lives in Sarasota?"

"Yes. That's the last time I saw the Plums. Before we moved."

"And that was in?"

"Ah . . . senior year at Vandersea. I was seventeen."

"So you haven't seen them since you were seventeen," Kelly Cruz said.

"No."

"But you said fifteen."

"Well, I didn't see much of them for a while before then."

"I understood that you were pretty good friends."

"Not really."

"I heard you used to sleep over sometimes. That seems like friends."

"I only did it a couple of times."

"When you were fifteen?"

"Yes."

The room seemed very quiet. Kimmy didn't look at Kelly Cruz. There was no longer any hint of cheerfulness. She suddenly seemed almost furtive. Kelly Cruz could feel a click inside, as if something had snapped into place, and a connection had been completed.

"What happened when you were fifteen?" Kelly Cruz said.

Kimmy looked at the floor and shook her head slowly.

"Something happened," Kelly Cruz said.

Kimmy kept shaking her head. Kelly Cruz paid no attention. She knew she was right.

"Florence Horvath died under suspicious circumstances," Kelly Cruz said. "Up in a town outside of Boston. I'm helping out on this end of the investigation."

Kimmy neither looked up nor stopped

the slow movement of her head.

"Before I came over here, I talked on the phone with the police chief up there. He said that maybe I should be alert for things involving Mr. Plum."

Kimmy stopped shaking her head. Her shoulders hunched up as if to protect her neck. Kelly Cruz had seen abused children before. She knew at a level she didn't understand that what happened had to do with sex.

"Did anything happen involving Mr. Plum?"

Kimmy stood and went to the bathroom and closed the door. Kelly Cruz heard the lock turn. She waited. Nothing happened. After a time she went to the bathroom door.

"Kimmy?" she said.

"Go away."

"Can't do that, Kimmy."

"I won't come out," Kimmy said.

"Sooner or later you will," Kelly Cruz said.

"I won't talk about it."

"You have to, Kimmy," Kelly Cruz said. "You want to spend the rest of your life with the door locked?"

Kelly Cruz waited. Kimmy didn't speak. The door didn't open.

"Kimmy?" Kelly Cruz said. "Are you all right?"

Silence.

"Kimmy, I have to know you're all right, and the only way I can know that is if you open the door and talk to me."

Silence.

"I'm concerned for your welfare," Kelly Cruz said. "Either you come out now, or I kick the door in. I'm a cop, I know how to do that."

Silence.

Kelly Cruz backed off two steps and drove her heel into the door next to the handle. She could hear the jam tear. The door slammed open and she went in. She didn't see Kimmy. She pulled the shower curtain aside. Kimmy was sitting in the tub with her knees up and her face pressed against them.

"Come on, Kimmy," Kelly Cruz said. "Get up."

Kimmy didn't move. Kelly Cruz bent over and put her hands under Kimmy's arms and tried to lift her.

"Up you go," Kelly Cruz said.

Kimmy was dead weight.

Kelly Cruz felt her neck. The pulse was okay. She was breathing. No sign that she had tried to hurt herself. She was just inert. Kelly Cruz tried again to lift her and failed.

"Shit," Kelly Cruz said.

She went to the living room and picked up the phone and called for help.

49

"Kimmy Young never told the Plum girls about Florence Horvath's death," Kelly Cruz said on the phone.

"So how'd they know?" Jesse said.

"I don't know," Kelly Cruz said. "But there's more."

"Okay."

"Kimmy and the twins used to be pals, and Kimmy would go and spend the night and listen to records and giggle about boys."

"Un-huh."

"When I asked her more about that she freaked out. I had to get the paramedics. We took her to the hospital and the doctors got her tranqued enough to be calm but not asleep and I talked with her."

Jesse felt hollow.

"Un-huh," he said.

"With drugs, she could talk about it. One night while she was there the old man molested them, and tried to include her."

"Shit," Jesse said.

"My thought exactly."

"She give you details?" Jesse said.

"Yes."

Jesse waited. He could hear Kelly Cruz breathing.

"I hate this," Kelly Cruz said.

"I don't like it much, either," Jesse said.

"They were all lying on a bed in the twins' bedroom, sideways, across it, you know. Looking at some snapshots, and he came in wearing his bathrobe and closed the door and sat on the bed with them and began to pat Kimmy and his bathrobe fell open and exposed him and Kimmy was like, paralyzed."

"How old?" Jesse said.

"Fifteen," Kelly Cruz said. "And he said he always kissed his girls good night and because she was a guest he'd kiss her, and he kissed the daughters and then her, with his tongue. And she started to cry and he put his hand under her skirt and she said no and clamped her legs and started to cry and he said maybe he could show her how easy it was, and he proceeded with the twins."

"Touching?" Jesse said.

"Fucking," Kelly Cruz said. "She wanted to run, she said, but she lived across town and she couldn't get home without a ride. And the twins were telling her not to be a baby and . . ."

"He did it," Jesse said.

"Yes."

"In front of his daughters," Jesse said.

"And when he got his rocks off, he got up and thanked her politely and left the room. She ran in and took a shower and got dressed, and called her father and he came and got her. She told him that she'd had a fight with the twins."

"How did the twins react to all of this?" Jesse said.

"Kimmy says that's part of what made it so awful. They seemed to take it in stride — so he banged you. He bangs us, too."

"She ever tell anyone?" Jesse said.

"No."

"She know if he molested Florence?" Jesse said.

"She doesn't know."

"But it's likely."

"Very," Kelly Cruz said.

"What happens to her now?"

"She'll spend the night," Kelly Cruz said. "Talk to a shrink tomorrow afternoon, and they'll decide."

"Notify her parents?"

"She doesn't want them to know."

"Maybe they should know anyway."

"This part of the case is mine, Jesse," Kelly Cruz said.

"And you are going to honor her wishes."

"I am."

Jesse was silent.

"I'll stay on it, and I'll keep you informed," Kelly Cruz said. "But I'm going to protect this kid as much as I can."

"It's the right thing to do," Jesse said.

"Thanks."

Again they were both quiet.

"There's something wrong with that man," Kelly Cruz said.

"Mr. Plum?"

"Yes. You haven't seen him. He's disconnected. You think maybe it's Alzheimer's or something, but he socializes. He plays tennis. He's not suffering dementia that I can see. Drinks a ton. They both do."

"Mr. and Mrs.?"

"Yes."

"You think she knows?"

"Yes."

"But doesn't know what to do?"

"That's my guess," Kelly Cruz said. "She said to me the other day that they had been gutted by wealth. Her phrase, *gutted.*"

"Money doesn't ruin people," Jesse said. "They ruin themselves. Money just helps them to spread the ruination around."

"I never had money," Kelly Cruz said.

"Me either, but I've seen it in action."

The soundless energy of the open phone line lingered between them as they sat silently for a long moment.

"You stay on it," Jesse said.

"I will," Kelly Cruz said.

"I thought it couldn't get worse," Jesse said.

"And now it has," Kelly Cruz said.

"Big time," Jesse said.

50

"Your problem," Dix said, "is you're scared."

"Of what?"

"Of the relationship. You were burned pretty badly, and now you are leery."

"Once burned," Jesse said.

"What's your biggest fear in the relationship?"

"I'll fuck up again, and lose her again."

Dix smiled.

"And if she fucks up?" he said.

Jesse frowned.

"Molly said almost the same thing," Jesse said. "For free."

"What did Molly say?"

"She said maybe the breakup was Jenn's fault."

Dix nodded.

"Was it?" Dix said.

"I guess in any breakup there's two people at fault."

"That sounds good," Dix said. "Do you believe it? Viscerally?"

"No. I'm pretty sure I drove her away."

Dix nodded and leaned his head back

261

and looked up at the ceiling for a moment. Then he looked at Jesse.

"You are co-opting the responsibility," Dix said. "Bad things happen. If it's your fault, then you can hope to prevent it in the future by not making the same mistake again. But if it is her fault, wholly, or partly, then you can't prevent it. You have to depend on her, wholly, or partly, to prevent it."

Jesse didn't say anything for a time. Dix waited. Jesse nodded to himself. Dix was right.

"It's about control," he said.

"You could think of it that way."

"And trust."

"If warranted," Dix said.

"And the sexualization stuff?" Jesse said. "That would be part of the control thing?"

Dix sighed.

"I think that's a paper tiger," Dix said. "I think you've clung to it as a way of keeping the responsibility. If you are ever-alert, and don't sexualize the relationship, then you won't lose her."

"So why we been talking about it?"

"I think you will be able to better integrate her past sexual indiscretions into your life," Dix said, "if you spend less time thinking about her in exclusively sexual terms. It might bring you some peace. But

I doubt that it was the cause of the breakup, or would cause one now. What you describe is mostly a healthy libido."

"It is?"

"Sure," Dix said, "and your fears have been exacerbated by the case you're working on in which control and loveless sexual objectification is rampant."

"And that's why the case matters so much."

"Probably," Dix said.

"So how do we fix this?"

"You stop being the way you are," Dix said.

"Like that?"

"Sure, like that. You think this is voodoo? If you're doing something self-destructive, sooner or later you have to decide to stop."

"So what the hell do you do?" Jesse said.

"I help get you to where you can stop."

"And you think I'm there?"

"Hell, yes," Dix said. "You are a tough guy. You can do what you decide you have to do. You'll either trust Jenn, or accept that you don't, and see what that brings."

Jesse nodded.

"So all you've done is get me ready," he said.

Dix smiled at him.

"Readiness is all," he said.

51

Two uniformed state troopers, one of them female, brought the Plum sisters into Jesse's office. Molly followed them in.

"Captain says we should wait for instructions from you," the male trooper said.

"What's your name?" Jesse said to the female trooper.

"Maura Quinlin."

"Maura, stick around here. Your partner can go."

"I'll be in the cruiser," the male trooper said.

He left.

"Sit," Jesse said, "please."

The sisters sat. Molly closed the office door and took a chair behind them. Trooper Quinlin sat beside her.

"Thanks for coming in," Jesse said.

"It was kind of cool," Corliss said.

"Riding in the police car and everything," Claudia said.

Jesse nodded.

"And the state police guy is a real

skunk," Corliss said.

"That like being a real fox?" Jesse said.

"Sure," Claudia said.

"People your age would probably call him a hunk," Corliss said.

Jesse nodded, looking at them. Corliss, it seemed to him, was usually the lead speaker. She'd say something and Claudia would follow up. He pointed at Corliss.

"Maura," he said to the female trooper, "take Corliss into the squad room and sit with her."

"What?" Corliss said.

"I have some heavy things to discuss," Jesse said. "With your sister."

"We always stay together," Corliss said.

"It won't be long," Jesse said. "Maura?"

Trooper Quinlin stood and put a hand under Corliss's right arm and helped her up.

"We always stay together," Claudia said.

"Not this time," Jesse said.

He nodded at Quinlin, who turned Corliss gently and walked her out of the office. Molly got up and closed the door behind them, and sat back down behind Claudia. Jesse looked at Claudia without speaking. Claudia smiled very brightly.

"We're twins, you know, we don't like to be separated," she said.

Jesse continued to look silently at Claudia.

"Did your father sexually molest you?" Jesse said.

Claudia stared at him. "What?"

"Did your father sexually molest you," Jesse said.

Claudia looked around the room as if Corliss might suddenly appear and answer the question. Jesse waited. Claudia stopped looking around and looked at him and opened her mouth and said nothing. Jesse waited. Claudia looked over her shoulder at Molly. Molly smiled at her but didn't speak.

"That's terrible," Claudia said finally.

"It is," Jesse said. "Did he molest you together or separately?"

Claudia shook her head.

"Did he molest all three of you together?"

"Three?"

"Florence, you and Corliss."

"Stop asking me that," Claudia said.

She began to cry. Jesse sat quietly and watched her. Behind Claudia, Molly sat looking at her hands, which were clasped in her lap. After a time Jesse took a box of Kleenex from a desk drawer and put it in front of Claudia, on the edge of his desk, where she could reach it.

"Let me define what I mean by molest," Jesse said. "So there won't be any confusion."

Claudia took one of the Kleenex and dabbed at her eyes.

"Did he touch you in a sexual way? Did he penetrate you?"

Claudia bent forward double and put her hands over her ears and began to moan. Jesse watched her quietly.

"For God's sake, Jesse," Molly said. "Leave the poor child alone."

"I need answers," Jesse said.

"Well, there are other ways," Molly said. "If you don't stop traumatizing her, I'll file a report with the selectmen."

Jesse grunted. He stood without a word and went out of the office. As he closed the door behind him he saw Molly get up and put her arm around Claudia's shoulder. Jesse smiled to himself. Then he went down into the squad room and closed the door.

Corliss and Maura Quinlin were sitting silently at the table. He sat down across from Corliss.

"Well," he said, "the truth is out."

"Excuse me?"

"About your father molesting you," Jesse said.

"Oh . . . my . . . God," Corliss said.

52

"The report to the selectmen line was inspired," Jesse said to Molly.

"I thought so," Molly said. "Made me look like really good cop at the same time it made you look like really bad cop."

"And cowardly," Jesse said.

Molly smiled faintly.

"You did scoot," Molly said, "as soon as you heard it."

They were quiet. Outside Jesse's window the early evening was starting to darken.

"I need a drink," Molly said.

Jesse nodded. He reached into the file cabinet where he kept it and brought out the bottle of Bushmill's. He poured some in a water glass and handed it to Molly.

"What are you going to tell your husband when you come staggering home with booze on your breath."

"I'll tell him I had to do some really pukey police work today," Molly said. "And I'll try not to stagger."

Molly drank from the glass and swallowed and put her head back and closed her eyes. She took a long breath. Jesse went to the refrigerator in the squad room and got a Coke and brought it back. Molly was still breathing deeply, with her eyes closed.

"What I hated the most," Molly said, "was the way they kept calling him Daddy and saying how he loved them."

"A way to keep it from killing them," Jesse said. "Thinking it's just Daddy loving you."

"How could anyone think that?"

"You think what you have to," Jesse said.

Molly sipped her whiskey.

"I wonder if Florence still thought her daddy loved her?"

Jesse shrugged.

"And if Daddy loved them so much," Molly said, "why did they have to bop everybody else they could find?"

"Looking for love?" Jesse said.

"That's love?"

"The only definition they had," Jesse said.

Molly sipped some whiskey.

"So," Molly said, "why wasn't Daddy enough?"

"Daddy was married," Jesse said.

"Jesus Christ," Molly said. "Oedipus?"

Jesse shrugged.

"I'm just talking," he said. "I don't know enough about it."

"The thought of sex with one of my children . . ." Molly shook her head. "I can't even think about it. It makes me numb even to try."

Jesse didn't speak.

"We had to know," Molly said.

Jesse nodded slowly. Molly drank again. The glass was empty. Jesse poured her a little more.

"But making them face it," Molly said. "It was . . ." She looked for a word. "Nauseating."

"We made them admit it," Jesse said. "They're a long way from facing it."

"You know the worst part?" Molly said.

She was staring down into her glass, looking at the caramel surface of the whiskey.

"When we brought them back together," Molly said. "And the fucking truth was sitting here in the room like some kind of ugly fucking toad and we're all staring at it, and they're both crying and saying, 'Don't tell Daddy. Don't tell Daddy.' "

Jesse nodded. Molly drank more of her whiskey.

"Daddy, for God's sake," Molly said. "Daddy."

"Daddy already knows," Jesse said.

"He doesn't know we know," Molly said.

"That's true," Jesse said.

"Like they've been bad little girls, telling on Daddy, tattletales," Molly said and drank. "Tattletales."

Jesse didn't speak. He had nothing to say in the face of Molly's overpowering maternity. He listened.

"And what about them now?" Molly said. "Back in the hotel after the day they spent with us? What happens to them?"

"They don't know anything they didn't know before," Jesse said.

"So what do they do?"

"My guess?" Jesse said. "Do some coke. Do some booze. Get laid. Giggle some."

Molly stared at him.

"God."

Jesse shrugged.

"That's how they've coped until now," he said.

"Jesse, these are twenty-year-old kids. They're five years older than my daughter."

"And they are depraved, stupid, careless, amoral people," Jesse said.

"They are victims."

"That may be," Jesse said. "But sympathizing with them is not my business. My business is catching the person who killed their sister."

"So why did you have to dig up all this awfulness?" Molly said.

"It was there," Jesse said. "I needed to know about it."

Molly held out her glass.

"One more," she said. "Then I'll go home and take a bath."

Molly wasn't a drinker. She was starting to slur her words. Jesse poured her another drink. She took a sip and looked at him over the glass. Her eyes had a sort of softness about them, the way Jenn's got if she drank too much.

"You are so nice," Molly said. "So often. And then . . . you are such a cynical, hard bastard."

"Nice guys finish last," Jesse said.

"Somebody said that."

"Leo Durocher."

"You know you don't believe it."

"Hell," Jesse said. "I've proved it."

Molly didn't say anything else. She sat quietly and finished her third drink. Jesse sipped his Coke.

When Molly's drink was gone, Jesse said, "Come on, hon, I'll drive you home."

"I can drive myself," she said.

"No," Jesse said. "You can't."

53

Rita Fiore's office offered a long view of the South Shore.

"Ms. Fiore will be right with you," the secretary said and left.

Jesse looked at the South Shore for a short while until Rita came in wearing a red suit and sat behind her desk.

"Wow," she said, "a coat and tie."

"Trying to fit in," Jesse said. "You talk to your private eye?"

"I did," Rita said.

She took a notebook from her middle drawer and opened it and thumbed through some pages.

"He gave me what he had."

"Didn't I run into him once?" Jesse said. "Working on something in Paradise?"

"I think so," Rita said.

"Him and a terrifying black guy."

"Terrifying is one description," Rita said. "Toothsome would be another."

Jesse smiled.

"What did he tell you?" he said.

Rita looked at her notes.

"They wanted to know if he could find a person and track his movements," Rita paused and studied her notes a moment.

"I hate my handwriting," she said. "And he said, 'You want someone followed?' and they said mostly they wanted to know where someone had been in the last few months. And he said that was possible, who did they have in mind?"

Rita looked up and smiled.

"Then they ran into a snag," Rita said. "The girls didn't want to tell him who."

"Whose movements they wanted him to discover?"

"That's right."

She returned to her notes and studied them for a moment.

"He said that it would be difficult to trace someone's movements if he didn't know who they were, and, he told me, 'They acted like they hadn't thought of that.' He told me, 'They kept looking at each other and silently agreeing that they couldn't give the name.' So he declined the employment offer . . . he claims, graciously."

"They give him any clue where he was supposed to look?" Jesse said.

"Miami and Boston," she said.

Rita looked at her notes.

"Miami or Boston," she said, "or travel between."

"Jesus Christ," Jesse said.

Rita waited. Jesse didn't say anything.

"I would guess," Rita said after a time of silence, "that I have provided you a clue."

"Yes," Jesse said.

They were quiet again.

Then Rita said, "I would guess that you are not going to share it with me."

"Also true," Jesse said.

"Because?"

"Because you are the best criminal defense lawyer in the state," Jesse said. "And you might end up defending someone I want convicted."

"Are you suggesting I would take unfair advantage of our, ah, relationship?"

"Yes."

Rita smiled.

"Well, of course," she said. "What are you going to do now?"

"I'm going to call Kelly Cruz," Jesse said.

"Who's Kelly Cruz?"

"Somebody I'm going to call," Jesse said.

Jesse stood. Rita stared at him for a moment.

"If I'd known you were like this," she said, "I'd never have bopped your socks off."

Jesse grinned at her.

"Yeah," he said. "You would have."

And they both began to laugh.

54

Back with the Plums, Kelly Cruz thought, as she sat on the same terrace, looking at the same blue-green water. Mr. and Mrs. Plum were both tanned and immaculate in white. The drink trolley was set up on the terrace. It was late afternoon and the cocktail hour had begun. *Probably been in effect for a while,* Kelly Cruz thought. She declined alcohol, and accepted a 7-Up.

"Just a few follow-up questions," Kelly Cruz said when they were all settled. "Have you been traveling at all in the last couple of months?"

"No, we haven't," Mr. Plum said pleasantly.

He smiled at Kelly Cruz. His eyes crinkled attractively when he smiled.

"Say, since the end of May?"

"No, we haven't," Mr. Plum said, just as pleasantly.

"Mrs. Plum?" Kelly Cruz said.

"No," she said. "I believe Willis drove up to Tallahassee, around the beginning of June, but I haven't gone anywhere."

"No, I didn't, Mommy," Mr. Plum said.

"You went up to visit the new store," Mrs. Plum said.

Mrs. Plum looked at Kelly Cruz.

"Willis loves to get in the car and drive off by himself. He drives all over the country."

"No," Mr. Plum was kind but firm, "you're confused."

Mrs. Plum looked at her husband. He was serene in his certainty, sipping a gin and tonic today. *Pacing himself,* Kelly Cruz thought.

"Didn't you open a new store in Tallahassee? Right after Memorial Day?"

Mr. Plum smiled fondly at his wife.

"Mommy, you're getting old on me. I didn't go anywhere in June."

"You have a car," Kelly Cruz said.

"My dear," Mr. Plum said. "Of course we do."

"Wow," Kelly Cruz said. "I never think of cars at a place like this. Is there a parking garage?"

"Indeed," Mr. Plum said. "And valet service all through the day and night."

He seemed proud.

"I suppose you have assigned spaces?" Kelly Cruz said. "Probably deeded."

She was aware as she chatted with Mr.

Plum that Mrs. Plum was staring at him. Mr. Plum looked at her indulgently.

"Of course," he said kindly.

He rang a small bell, and the Cuban maid came in and brought the Plums another drink from the trolley. Kelly Cruz nursed her 7-Up. As he sipped his new drink, Mr. Plum seemed to lose interest in Kelly Cruz. Instead he looked thoughtfully out from the patio at Biscayne Bay. Mrs. Plum appeared not to look at anything.

"Well," Kelly Cruz said. "So, no travel, I guess."

Mr. Plum seemed not to hear her. Mrs. Plum shrugged and shook her head.

Kelly Cruz put her unfinished soft drink on the coffee table and stood.

"Well, thanks, sorry to bother you," she said.

Mr. Plum continued to look at the bay. Mrs. Plum reached forward and rang the bell, and the Cuban maid came and showed Kelly Cruz to the door.

Kelly Cruz paused at the door and smiled at the maid, *just a couple of palsy Cuban girls taking a moment to chat.*

"Mi hermana," Kelly Cruz said. "You remember when Mr. Plum went up to Tallahassee a couple of months ago?"

"Yes ma'am."

"Mrs. Plum didn't go with him, did she?" Kelly Cruz said.

"No ma'am."

"Good," Kelly Cruz said. "Thanks, Magdalena. The garage on the lower level?"

"Yes ma'am."

55

Jesse was on the phone with Kelly Cruz.

"He's so empty and sweet," she said. "It's like part of him is missing but he doesn't mind and there's no reason you should be upset about it."

"Except for him being a pedophile."

"Except for that," Kelly Cruz said.

"And you think the wife knows," Jesse said.

"She knows," Kelly Cruz said. "I can't promise you that she even knows she knows."

"But she knows."

"She knows," Kelly Cruz said.

"Can you work on her?"

"Some. If I can catch her away from him. They are nearly always together, as far as I can tell."

"Contentment," Jesse said. "After years of marriage."

"Except for him being a pedophile," Kelly Cruz said.

"Except for that," Jesse said.

"How about the maid?"

"See no evil, speak no evil."

"Not even for a sister?"

"She doesn't care if I'm of pure Cathtilian heritage," Kelly Cruz said. "She's got a good job and she won't do anything to risk it. I had to trick her to say anything."

"Any other servants?"

"Houseman and a cook. They are much less forthcoming than the maid."

"So the servants are a dead end," Jesse said.

"Complete," Kelly Cruz said. "However, being a stubborn broad, I check out the parking garage. The attendant doesn't remember whether Mister took his car out or not at the beginning of June. So I say, Is it there now? And he says it is and shows it to me. Actually I say this all in Spanish."

"Muy simpatico," Jesse said.

"Si," Kelly Cruz said. "It's an Escalade. Black. Loaded. I checked it out. It told me nothing. But I did see a small E-ZPass transponder inside the windshield."

"New York," Jesse said. "Our system works with it, too."

"Lot of them do, along the East Coast," Kelly Cruz said. "Then I called the new Plum and Partridge store in Tallahassee, and *yes*, they opened the day after Memorial Day, and *no*, Mr. Plum didn't attend.

No one at the store that I talked to even knows what he looks like. I gather he's not a hands-on manager."

"But you are convinced he went somewhere," Jesse said.

"Yes. Mrs. Plum shut up once he made it clear he would deny it," Kelly Cruz said. "But he wasn't home the first few days in June."

"So if I tracked down the hits on his E-ZPass transponder, maybe I'd learn something," Jesse said.

"If he drove someplace where the system is in effect," Kelly Cruz said.

"And at worst I'd learn what I already know," Jesse said.

"Which is?"

"Next to *nada.*"

"Wow," Kelly Cruz said. "You really do speak our language."

"I used to work in L.A.," Jesse said.

"Sorry to hear that," Kelly Cruz said.

56

"Your guest is already here," Daisy Dyke told Jesse. "Hoo ha."

"Hoo ha?" Jesse said.

"Wasn't a married woman I might take a run at her m'self."

"I think she's on my side of the fence," Jesse said.

"Never know till you try," Daisy said. "You taking a run?"

"No. It's business."

Blondie Martin was at a table in the back of Daisy's beside the bar, drinking Lillet on the rocks. Daisy held the chair out for Jesse and pushed it in as he sat.

"So," Blondie said, when Daisy had left them. "How come you're not grilling me in the back room of the station house."

"I was afraid you'd like it too much," Jesse said.

"Especially with handcuffs," Blondie said.

The waitress appeared. Jesse ordered iced tea. Blondie asked for another Lillet.

"No drinking on duty?" Blondie said.

"Or off," Jesse said.

"You ever drink?"

"I did."

"Are you an alcoholic?"

"I don't know," Jesse said. "At the moment, I'm not drinking."

The waitress brought their drinks, and took their order for lunch.

"So what do you want with me, Chief Yokel?" Blondie said. "You been watching me in the video?"

"I've worn it out," Jesse said. "But today I'd like to talk about Darnell."

"Harrison? Why talk about Harrison when we can talk about me?"

"This is a working lunch," Jesse said. "What is Harrison's attraction for women?"

"Money," Blondie said.

"That what appeals to you?" Jesse said.

"Sure," Blondie said.

"Anything else?"

"Well, I mean money can only buy you so much. Some of these freakos are scary. Harrison isn't. He's kinky, yes. But if you aren't kinky in the same way, he doesn't insist."

"Is he jealous?"

"Of what?" Blondie said.

"Any of his women being with other men?"

"Oh God, no," Blondie said. "This is recreational, Jesse. Nobody gets jealous or possessive or anything."

She grinned at him and finished her first Lillet.

"We just all like to fuck," she said.

Jesse smiled.

"Doesn't make you a bad person," Jesse said.

Blondie didn't laugh.

"Actually, I am sort of a bad person," she said. "I'm shallow and careless, pretty selfish. But I try to be honest."

"That why you told me that Darnell was lying about the two crewmen in the video with Florence?"

"Oh hell, I don't know," Blondie said. "You looked pretty good on the boat. I thought it might be fun to see how good you were in bed."

"So it was a seduction ploy," Jesse said.

"Yeah," Blondie said. "See what I mean? I ratted out Harrison, just because you looked like you might be hot."

Jesse nodded. The waitress delivered lunch. A tongue sandwich on light rye for Jesse. Something called a California Salad for Blondie. Blondie ordered a bottle of Chardonnay.

"Was Florence Darnell's favorite?"

"I don't think so," Blondie said.

"I was told she was and that he ditched her for you."

Blondie Martin looked at Jesse with blank astonishment.

"Ditched her? For me?"

Jesse nodded. Blondie stared.

"Harrison's favorite," Blondie said, "was whoever gave him his most recent BJ."

"Well," Jesse said. "It's a standard."

"The only way this whole deal works on the boat is that absolutely nobody aboard cares about anything but their own orgasm," Blondie said.

"Including the high-school girls he recruits locally?" Jesse said.

"Sure. You think they're out there looking for love?"

"Maybe," Jesse said.

"Oh, fuck the shrink shit," Blondie said. "They are out there to get laid."

"Like you," Jesse said.

"Like me," Blondie said, "and have some laughs and a good time and maybe come away with a little jing."

"So why did Florence send him the videotape?"

"She sent it?"

"Didn't she?"

"I don't know who sent it. I picked up

our mail in town that day. There was no return address. When I gave it to Harrison he wondered who sent it."

"Did you see it?"

"Sure, we watched it together. It was cool. Harrison especially got a kick out of it. Wanted to try it with me. But . . ." Blondie shook her head.

"And he wasn't upset by it?"

"No, of course not. What's to be upset about. He loved it."

"So when did it arrive? Can you remember?"

"While Florence was off the boat."

"Off the boat?"

"Yeah."

"So when was the last time you saw her?" Jesse said.

"She came up with us on the boat from Florida."

"This trip?"

"Yeah, sure," Blondie said.

"And everybody on the boat saw her."

"Sure."

Blondie sipped her wine. She hadn't, Jesse noticed, eaten much of her California Salad.

"And everyone lied about it," Jesse said.

"Of course we lied," Blondie said. "We didn't want anybody snooping around into our lifestyle."

"So how come you are talking to me now?" Jesse said.

Blondie shrugged.

"I like you. I want to impress you. I'm drinking. I feel like it."

"So how did she die?" Jesse said. "You know that, too?"

"No. She went ashore for a few days. Said her daddy was in town. The tape arrived while she was gone. I remember Harrison being excited to watch it with her and asking when she'd be back."

"And it was mailed from Miami," Jesse said.

"I didn't notice," Blondie said. "But that's what Harrison told me."

"So if she were really here with her daddy," Jesse said, "she couldn't have mailed it to him."

"Somebody could have mailed it for her," Blondie said.

She poured herself some wine.

"Why would she go to that trouble?" Jesse said.

"Haven't got the foggiest," Blondie said. "You're the damn master detective."

"Yeah," Jesse said. "That would be me."

He sat and looked at the second half of his sandwich. Blondie drank some wine.

"Do you remember when she went

ashore to see her father?" Jesse said.

"Nope," Blondie said. "No idea really. You know, Florence wasn't a big deal to me."

Blondie picked up a small tangerine segment from her California Salad and ate it.

"How was she when she came back?" Jesse said.

Blondie drank some wine and swallowed, pursed her lips and looked at the corner of the room for a moment.

"I don't think she came back," Blondie said.

57

"E-ZPass transponder number you gave me," Healy said, "belonging to Willis Plum of Miami?"

"Yeah."

"Was used between June first and June fourth in Maryland and Delaware and Jersey and New York, and in the Fast Lane entrances on the Mass Pike inbound at Sturbridge and at Brighton. It was used going the other way between June seventh and twelfth."

"Why would he have an E-ZPass transponder, living in Miami?" Jesse said.

"Lot of people who drive to New York a lot have them," Healy said. "Nice to zip past the tollbooth backups."

"And our system works with theirs," Jesse said.

"Convenient," Healy said.

Jesse and Healy leaned on the iron railing at the edge of the pier above the float where the small boats docked. In the dark water along the edge of the wharf, an occasional dead fish floated, and orange peels, and indestructible bits of Styrofoam, scraps of seaweed, an occasional crab shell, one condom, and a red-and-white bobber that had come loose from a fishing line.

"Found her right there," Jesse said. "Against the float."

"With the other flotsam," Healy said.

"Fancy word," Jesse said.

"Yeah. Sometimes I read things."

They were quiet, watching the slow water slap gently at the pier. Jesse raised his eyes and looked at the mouth of the harbor. He thought he could pick out the *Lady Jane* anchored there. He took in a big breath and let it out slowly.

"Maybe I should reformulate my theory of the case," Jesse said.

"What would your new formulation be?" Healy said.

"That I don't know what the fuck is going on and I don't know who to believe and I have been chasing my own ass up to now."

"You know this business," Healy said. "You have to assume everyone's lying to you. But you have to act as if they weren't."

"The bastard was up here," Jesse said.

"His car was up here," Healy said.

"She went ashore to see him and never came back."

"Blondie says."

"Why would she lie," Jesse said, "about this."

Healy smiled.

"Yeah," Jesse said. "She'd lie about the time of day if it seemed like a fun thing. Or she had an itch she felt like scratching."

"Still," Healy said. "He probably was here. He is probably a pedophile. He probably molested his daughters. He's a lying bastard. What's Cruz think of him."

"She thinks there's something really wrong with him."

Healy smiled.

"I'll bet she's right," he said.

"So why would he decide all of a sudden to drive up here and kill her?"

"If that's what he decided," Healy said.

"I know," Jesse said. "I know. I can't prove it yet. But let's assume he killed her."

"Okay," Healy said.

"Why would he suddenly drive up here and kill her and drive home?"

"Maybe she told him it had to stop," Healy said. "Her, the twin sisters, all of it."

"As far as I know she came up with Darnell from Miami, so she was around there before June. Maybe they had the falling out then."

"And she left in a huff and came north with Darnell," Healy said.

"And he decided to follow her."

"Why not kill her right there, during the falling-out moment?" Healy said.

"Maybe it was in front of the mother and he couldn't do it then."

"She knows, you think?" Healy said.

"Cruz says she does."

"She know he killed their daughter, assuming he did?" Healy said.

"I don't know. It might be a nice piece of leverage to shake her loose."

"Course, your original theory might actually be true," Healy said. "Darnell, or Ralston, or both."

"Or they've just been lying every step of the way because they're afraid of getting caught in the sex ring stuff."

"Most of which is not illegal."

"True," Jesse said. "But it is not universally popular in the best yacht clubs."

"Everybody has things to cover up in this thing," Healy said.

"Most things," Jesse said.

Healy grinned at him.

"Ah, Laddy Buck," Healy said. "The job is making you cynical."

"Anyway, I've got them on the stat rape charge," Jesse said.

"Nice to have a fallback position," Healy said.

Jesse smiled for a moment.

"At least I can arrest somebody," he said.

58

"We're going to have to talk to the Plum twins again," Jesse said to Molly. "Can you stay sober long enough to sit in?"

Molly blushed.

"Shut up," she said.

"Let's have a little respect here," Jesse said.

"Shut up, Chief Stone," Molly said.

Jesse nodded.

"Better," he said. "Get Steve to cover the desk."

"We doing good cop, bad cop again?"

"Play it by ear," Jesse said. "But it doesn't do any harm if they like you and fear me."

"They bring a lawyer?" Molly said.

"Nope."

"Wow," Molly said. "They are dumb."

"I'm counting on it," Jesse said.

The twins sat beside each other in front of Jesse's desk. Molly sat as she had before, behind them, near the door.

"We want to stay together," Corliss said.

Jesse looked at them without expression.

"Maybe I can get you adjoining cells at Framingham," Jesse said.

"Framingham?" Claudia said.

"Women's Reformatory," Molly said behind them.

They both turned toward her.

"Jail?" Corliss said.

"We might go to jail?" Claudia said.

"It happens," Molly said. "If you don't let us help you. It could happen."

Jesse glared at Molly.

"What are we, the Salvation Army?" he said.

"Part of our job is to help people," Molly said.

"I don't want to help them," Jesse said. "I want to put them in jail."

Both girls turned back toward Jesse. He could see Molly behind them, while they weren't looking, take a deep breath. *I know,* Jesse thought, *I know.*

"You have lied to me," Jesse said to the girls, "every time you could, since the first time I talked with you."

"We didn't do anything, like a crime," Corliss said.

Jesse let his chair tip forward. He stood and came around his desk and bent from the waist and put his face an inch away from Corliss's face.

"I don't like you," he said. "I hate every-thing you are. So you keep sitting there lying to me, it makes me happy. It makes it easier and easier for me to put your degen-erate asses in jail for ten years."

"Leave her alone," Claudia said.

Jesse shifted his face a half inch toward her.

"Both of you," he said.

"We're not lying," Corliss said. "We haven't even said anything."

"You don't know that your father was up here in June," Jesse said.

Both of them said "Ohmigod" at the same time.

"You didn't feel like you should tell me that, huh?" Jesse said.

"Jesse," Molly said. "They're kids."

Jesse raised his eyes and stared at Molly.

"I'm getting sick of the bleeding heart, missy," he said. "You don't like how I question suspects, you can leave right now."

"I can't leave them in here alone with you, for God's sake," Molly said.

"Then button it up," Jesse said.

"If I have to go to the selectmen, I will," Molly said.

"Fuck the selectmen. I nail these two de-generates, they'll give me a raise."

"Did Daddy kill Florence?" Corliss said.

Jesse was still for a moment. The anger left his face. Then he straightened and rested his butt against the edge of his desk, and folded his arms. His voice was gentle when he spoke.

"You think?" he said.

"We were afraid of it," Claudia said. "It's why we came here and why we wanted to get a private detective."

"To whom you wouldn't reveal a name."

"We got too scared," Corliss said.

"Of Daddy?" Jesse said.

"Yes," Claudia said.

"If he found out," Corliss said.

Jesse nodded.

"Let's run over that videotape you made of your sister and the two guys," Jesse said.

"It was for Daddy," Claudia said.

Jesse could hear Molly exhale. He nodded softly.

"Okay," he said. "Okay."

He went around the desk and sat down.

"She hated Daddy," Corliss said. "She said this was her kissing him off."

"And she sent him the tape?"

"A duplicate," Claudia said. "She had a bunch of duplicates made. I think she was going to keep sending them to him, you know? Every month? Drive him crazy?"

They both spoke rapidly, the words flowing out as if through the widening crack in a dam.

"So how did a copy end up on Harrison Darnell's boat?" Jesse said.

"We talked about that," Corliss said. "Me and Claud. We thought maybe Florence brought a copy to show him. Harrison liked stuff like that."

"I think it was mailed from Miami," Jesse said.

"That's the other thing we thought," Claudia said.

"Which was?" Jesse said.

"Maybe Daddy sent it," Corliss said.

"Why would he do that?"

"Daddy's odd sometimes," Claudia said.

"We thought maybe he sent it to Harrison to embarrass Flo," Corliss said.

"He didn't know that it wouldn't?" Jesse said.

"I think he thought Flo had a nice upper-class wealthy beau," Claudia said.

"He thought we did, too," Corliss said.

"What were you afraid Daddy would do if he found out you had hired a private detective to investigate him?" Jesse said.

"We thought he'd kill us," Claudia said.

She looked at Corliss. They both nodded.

"Who told you about your sister's death?" Jesse said.

"Mom," Corliss said.

"So why did you tell me Kimmy Young told you?"

"Kimmy?" Claudia said.

"We told you Kimmy?" Corliss said.

"Yep."

"God, why would we do that?" Claudia said.

"That was what sort of tore the cover off," Jesse said.

"We were scared," Corliss said. "I guess we just said a name."

"We were afraid if we told you Mom, that would sort of lead you to Daddy," Claudia said.

"Because you didn't want to get him in any trouble," Jesse said.

"Yes," Corliss said.

"We love him," Claudia said.

"And he loves us," Corliss said.

"And you were afraid he might kill you," Jesse said.

"Daddy gets so mad sometimes," Claudia said.

They looked at each other again and nodded.

59

Kelly Cruz met Jesse at the gate in the Miami airport. She had a short black haircut and a wide mouth and nice posture. Her ass was, in fact, perky. She was wearing white heels and white slacks and a blue linen jacket and holding a handmade sign that said STONE. Jesse was glad that she was good-looking. They shook hands and he followed her outside where they got into a maroon Crown Victoria parked under a no-parking sign in front of the terminal. Kelly Cruz got into the front beside the driver. Jesse got in back.

"Jesse Stone," Kelly Cruz said. "Raymond Ortiz."

The driver turned and said hello.

"Raymond works Homicide," she said. "Here in Miami."

"Nice to have an official presence," Jesse said. "In case we want to arrest somebody."

"That's me," Ortiz said. "Official presence."

"How you want to handle this?" Kelly Cruz said as they headed east from the airport on the Dolphin Expressway.

"My usual approach," Jesse said, "is to blunder in and shake the sack and see what falls out."

"Works for me," Ortiz said.

"It's your case," Kelly Cruz said.

"But you know the people," Jesse said. "Got a suggestion?"

"The wife's ready to pop," Kelly Cruz said. "The old man is buried so deep inside somewhere that I got no clue on him."

"And the help's nowhere," Jesse said.

Kelly Cruz shook her head.

"Nowhere," she said. "Working for the Yankee dollar. Got no other interest."

"You're Cuban," Jesse said.

"My mother is," Kelly Cruz said.

"And Raymond."

"Si," Raymond said in a parody Latino accent.

"And that doesn't help."

"Not a bit," Kelly Cruz said. "About as much as you being a gringo will help with the Plums."

"Gringo?" Jesse said.

"I'm trying to sound authentic," Kelly Cruz said. "I was you I'd go for the mother, and how the pervert killed her daughter."

Jesse nodded. Kelly Cruz glanced at her watch.

"Eleven-fifty," she said. "They'll be drinking by the time we get there."

"Good or bad?" Jesse said.

"Doesn't seem to have much effect," Kelly Cruz said.

"We're expected," Jesse said.

"We are, if they remember," Kelly Cruz said.

The valet service knew a cop when they saw one. Nobody offered to take the Crown Vic, and nobody objected when Ortiz parked it right in front of the main entrance and got out. In the lobby, Ortiz showed his badge to the concierge. She called upstairs, and when they got out of the elevator at the penthouse, the maid was waiting for them at the front door of the Plums' vast condo. She led them through the unruffled living room to the terrace where the drink trolley had been wheeled into place, and a small buffet was set up.

Mrs. Plum, in a frothy ankle-length turquoise dress, was reclining on a chaise. Mr. Plum, wearing a white shirt and white linen slacks, sat erect in his chair near her head. Both were drinking Manhattans. Jesse stared at the father. *You son of a bitch.*

60

Ortiz's only duty was to add jurisdictional presence where Jesse and Kelly Cruz had none. They declined to eat. Ortiz accepted a large plateful of assorted tea sandwiches and ate them quietly, leaning his hips against the railing of the terrace, and sipping mango iced tea from a glass he balanced on the top rail. Kelly Cruz sat opposite the Plums in a white satin chair with no arms. Jesse remained standing.

"Chief of police," Willis Plum said. "That's quite an achievement."

Jesse ignored him.

"Mrs. Plum," he said. "A while ago you told Detective Cruz your husband had taken a trip at the beginning of June, and it appeared that you were mistaken."

"I often am," Mrs. Plum said, in a tone that didn't mean it.

"Good news," Jesse said. "You were right. He didn't go to Tallahassee. But he was in the Boston area the first week in June."

She looked quickly at her husband.

"I knew I was right," she said.

Mr. Plum shook his head.

"He's wrong, Mommy," Plum said gently, "just like you were."

"He has an E-ZPass transponder on his car," Jesse said. "It's compatible with the Fast Lane system in Massachusetts. He was driving on the Massachusetts Turnpike the first week in June."

"Transponder," she said.

"The car goes through the no-toll lane and is electronically recorded. Toll is charged to your credit card."

"The thing on the windshield," Mrs. Plum said.

"It is useful almost everywhere north of Washington," Mr. Plum said. "I drive often to New York. It is a great timesaver."

Jesse showed no sign that Mr. Plum had spoken.

"So when you thought he was off to Tallahassee to open the new store," Jesse said to Mrs. Plum, "he was, in fact, driving up to Boston to see Florence."

Mr. Plum spoke in the same gentle voice.

"What he's saying is wrong, Mommy."

She stared at him for a moment. He sat very erect, his ankles together. He drank his Manhattan carefully and patted his lips with a napkin. Jesse thought he looked prim.

"Mommy," Mr. Plum said.

"Do you have any theory, Mrs. Plum," Jesse said, "why he went up there?"

"No," she said.

"Do you have any theory on why he pretends he didn't?"

"I never went, Mommy."

Mrs. Plum didn't look at her husband. She kept her gaze fixed on Jesse.

"No," Mrs. Plum said. "I don't."

The room was silent. The sky was very blue above the terrace. The bay beyond the terrace looked clean and bright.

"I didn't do anything wrong," Mr. Plum said.

Mrs. Plum stared at Jesse. Jesse walked over to the railing and leaned on it beside Ortiz. Mr. Plum poured himself a Manhattan from a silver shaker beaded with moisture. He offered the shaker to Mrs. Plum who shook her head. She sipped from her still-sufficient glass.

"I didn't do anything wrong," Mr. Plum said.

Ortiz ate his sandwiches. Kelly Cruz sat with her legs crossed, her hands clasped over her right knee. Jesse waited. No one spoke. Slowly Mrs. Plum shifted her gaze from Jesse to her husband. He smiled at her.

He said, "It's going to be all right, Mommy."

She continued to look at him. He sat calmly with his Manhattan delicately held with thumb and forefinger. His face was toward her, but he didn't appear to be looking at anything.

"You are a monstrous pig of a man," Mrs. Plum said to him.

Her voice was calm and the tone was simply the assertion of an obvious fact.

"Mommy," he said, "please. Not in front of guests."

"You killed her," Mrs. Plum said. "Didn't you."

"Mommy," he said again in his pleasant detached way, "please let's mind our manners."

"She sent you the tape and you went into a jealous frenzy and drove up there and killed her."

"Tape?" Mr. Plum said.

"You think I don't know about the tape? You think I didn't recognize her handwriting when it came? You think I didn't find it in your study while you were out? You think I didn't play it? You think I don't know about you?"

Her voice went slowly, almost ploddingly, up the scale until she was almost screaming.

"That tape was private," Mr. Plum said.

"Private?" Mrs. Plum's voice was down into calm again. "That is my daughter."

"And mine," Mr. Plum said. He seemed still to be looking at nothing. "It was private between me and my daughter."

"Whom you have been fucking since she was thirteen," Mrs. Plum said.

Mr. Plum suddenly looked at her.

"Mommy," he said firmly, "don't be crude."

She stared at him and then looked at Jesse and Ortiz, then at Kelly Cruz.

"He's been doing it since they were little girls," she said to Kelly Cruz. "All three of them. We never talked about it. Maybe he thought I didn't know, but I knew."

"And did nothing?" Kelly Cruz said.

"He had money and we were well situated," Mrs. Plum said. "He made no demands on me. It was easier to drink."

"Not for the girls," Kelly Cruz said.

"I loved those girls," Mr. Plum said. "And they loved me."

"And you destroyed them," Mrs. Plum said. "And now you've killed Florence."

"Betsy," Mr. Plum said. "Please. Can't

this wait until our guests have departed?"

Mrs. Plum finished her Manhattan. With no apparent thought, Mr. Plum refilled her glass. She began to cry silently.

"See him," she gasped. "See him? That's what he's like. He's like a reptile. He doesn't hear. He doesn't feel. He has no body warmth."

Kelly Cruz nodded.

"I am not a reptile, Betsy," Plum said. "I am a man with the feelings and impulses of my gender."

"And you killed Florence," Mrs. Plum said.

Her voice was beginning to soar again.

"You killed Florence because you were jealous that she was having sex with other people."

"The tape was insulting," Mr. Plum said.

"And you killed her."

"She betrayed me, Betsy."

"And you killed her," Mrs. Plum said. "Say it. Say you killed her. Say something for once in your weird reptilian existence, say something true. Say . . . you . . . killed . . . her!"

"You can't know," Mr. Plum said. "None of you can know how I loved those girls."

"Which is . . . why you . . . killed her?"

Mrs. Plum struggled to speak.

"You . . . loved her so . . . much . . . you killed her?"

"I killed her to keep her from becoming worse than she had become," Mr. Plum said. "I really had no choice."

He picked up the silver shaker, found that it was empty, put it down and rang the little bell for the maid.

61

Kelly Cruz turned her drink slowly on the bar in front of her. She was drinking Jack Daniel's on the rocks.

"So what about Darnell and Ralston?" she said to Jesse.

They were sitting at the bar in Jesse's hotel. Jesse was drinking a Virgin Mary. Kelly Cruz had on a black dress with spaghetti straps and a skirt that stopped above her knees. She had a nice tan. A small black purse lay on the bar beside her drink.

"We busted them yesterday, for statutory rape."

"Will it hold in court?"

"We got Darnell on videotape."

"Righteous tape?"

"Absolutely."

"How about Ralston?"

"If our witness holds," Jesse said.

"She might not?"

Jesse shrugged.

"She's a kid," he said.

"Think they'll do time?"

"Not my area," Jesse said.

"What do you think?" Kelly Cruz said. "Cop to cop."

Jesse smiled.

"I don't think about that," he said. "Too many variables. How good is their lawyer? How good is the prosecutor? Will their sexual history be admitted? Will they plead out?"

"Probably," Kelly Cruz said.

Jesse nodded.

"No jail time," Kelly Cruz said.

Jesse shrugged.

"I arrest, they prosecute," he said.

Kelly Cruz looked at Jesse's Virgin Mary.

"Drinking problem?" she said.

"Yes."

"How long you been sober?"

"I haven't had a drink going onto a year," Jesse said.

"Miss it?"

"Yes."

"My husband was a drunk," Kelly Cruz said.

"You divorced?"

Kelly Cruz nodded.

"Know where he is now?"

"No," Kelly Cruz said.

"How are the kids?"

"Good," she said. "Two boys. We live

with my parents. My father's a good father for all of us."

Jesse finished his Virgin Mary and gestured for another one.

"No wonder you got a problem," Kelly Cruz said. "You'll drink a lot of anything."

"Vitamin C," Jesse said as the bartender set the new drink in front of him.

"Why do you suppose Willis Plum sent the videotape of his daughter to Darnell?"

Jesse shook his head.

"He's way past anything I understand," Jesse said.

"Maybe he thought it would embarrass her," Kelly Cruz said.

Jesse nodded.

"Maybe he was sending it to her, you know, dismissing it by returning it," Kelly Cruz said.

"Blondie Martin says it was addressed to Darnell."

"Maybe he did it because he's a whack job," Kelly Cruz said.

"Not such a whack job that he flew up there and left a paper trail with the airlines," Jesse said.

Kelly Cruz drank some bourbon.

"You going home tomorrow?" Kelly Cruz said.

"Yeah. Paperwork's done. I'm supposed

to take him back with me."

"Got anyone waiting?" Kelly Cruz said.

"My ex-wife," Jesse said.

"You have an ex-wife waiting for you?"

"We're trying to rework things," Jesse said.

"How's that going?"

"So far," Jesse said, "so good."

"Plum girls are home, staying with their mother," Kelly Cruz said.

"Good," Jesse said.

"Think anything good will happen to them?" Kelly Cruz said.

"Probably not," Jesse said.

"Father's gone," Kelly Cruz said. "They're with their mother."

"Who is not a real lot better than their father," Jesse said.

"No," Kelly Cruz said.

"You did a hell of a job on this," Jesse said.

"I know."

"A lot of it on your own time, I suspect."

"Some," Kelly Cruz said. "On the other hand, I met a nice marina manager, and a very fine private pilot."

"Good," Jesse said. "I'm glad you profited from the experience."

Kelly Cruz finished her drink and stood.

"Got a date with the pilot," she said.

"It's his turn. The marina manager has already profited from the experience."

Jesse stood. He left his Virgin Mary half consumed on the bar.

"Thanks, Kell," he said. "You're a hell of a cop."

She turned toward him and gave him a light kiss on the mouth.

"You're pretty good at the job yourself," she said. "Good luck with the ex-wife."

"And you with the pilot," Jesse said.

Kelly Cruz stiffened her upper lip over her teeth and did an imitation of somebody. *Bogart,* Jesse thought. *Maybe.*

"Ain't a matter of luck, blue eyes," she said, and picked up her purse.

With her left hand she patted his cheek. He put his hand over hers for a moment. She was wearing a really nice perfume. They stood for a moment like that, then she took her hand away and he stood and watched her walk out of the bar.

If there's luck involved, it'll be the pilot's.

62

It was cool and rainy in Paradise. The boats were gone. The harbor was back to its normal maritime clutter. Jenn had made a meatloaf, and baked two potatoes. Jesse had tossed a salad. They sat now at the small table in the kitchen and ate supper together. Jenn opened a bottle of Riesling.

"Aren't you supposed to have red wine with meatloaf?" Jesse said.

"I think with meatloaf you can have what you want," Jenn said.

"That's one of the good things about meatloaf," Jesse said.

"Another being that I know how to make it," Jenn said.

The apartment was quiet. Through the open door to the balcony they could hear the rain fall.

"I think we're doing good," Jenn said after a time.

"Yes."

"How are you?" Jenn said.

"Good."

"And that hideous case is over," Jenn said.

317

"For me," Jesse said.

Jenn nodded.

"Do you actually know what happened?"

"Sort of," Jesse said.

"One thing I wondered ever since you told me," Jenn said. "Why did the twins tell you it was what's her name? Kimmy something?"

"Kimmy Young," Jesse said.

"If they had made up a name, or told the truth, you might never have figured it out."

"That's right," Jesse said.

"You think at some level they did it on purpose?"

"Probably."

"Because they wanted you to figure it out?"

"Probably."

"And stop it," Jenn said.

"Which I did," Jesse said.

"Do you know how Florence died?"

"Sort of," Jesse said.

Jenn waited.

"For whatever reason, after all this time," Jesse said, "Florence decided to stop being Daddy's girl. They had some kind of confrontation about it. The old man never quite says. And she went off and made the video with her sisters and sent it to him."

"Some kind of perverted kiss-off," Jenn said.

"I guess," Jesse said. "He sent it on to Darnell. Plum never quite told me why. Then, he says, he drove up here to reconcile. They always liked sailing, the mother says. So Florence rented a boat, packed a picnic, and they went off for a romantic sail, during which time they argued, and he threw her in the water, and sailed off."

"And he didn't know where she'd gotten the boat so he just put it the first place he saw."

"Probably," Jesse said.

"God, it's like a lovers' quarrel," Jenn said.

"Except he was careful to give himself a cover story and drive all the way so there'd be no record of him with the airlines."

Jenn put her fork down and looked at Jesse for a long silent moment.

"Which means he planned to do it before he left," Jenn said.

"Un-huh."

"My God," Jenn said.

Jesse didn't say anything.

"The other daughters?"

"Home with Mom," Jesse said.

"You think they'll get over this?"

"No."

Jenn poured herself some wine.

"So he's destroyed all his children," Jenn said.

"And his wife let him," Jesse said.

"How could she deny so much," Jenn said.

"She needed to, I guess."

Jenn took a sip of her wine.

"Have you talked with Dix about this?"

"Indirectly," Jesse said.

"You've talked to him about how this affected you."

"Yes."

"Want to tell me?"

"It was so much about sex and so little about love," Jesse said. "And I was already worried that with you I'm too much about sex anyway."

Jenn listened without comment. Jesse went on.

"Dix says that it's a kind of, what did he call it, amulet, I've created. If what I do can cause us to break up again, then the control is with me, because I can change. If it's things you do . . ." Jesse shrugged.

"I guess you need to trust me a little more," Jenn said. "Even if my track record isn't so good."

"It's about both of us," Jesse said. "Maybe I need to trust us both."

Jenn smiled and sipped some wine.

Jesse watched her. "It's been a year," he said.

"I know."

"I think I'll try a glass of wine," Jesse said.

"Like that?" Jenn said.

Jesse nodded.

"Maybe two," he said.

"You think you should?" Jenn said. "You think you can?"

"Only one way to find out."

"What if you can't?"

"Then I'll stop again," Jesse said. "I've proved I can do that."

"Have you talked to Dix about this?" Jenn said.

"Indirectly," Jesse said.

Jenn looked at Jesse's wineglass and grinned suddenly. He liked it when she grinned.

"You sure you want to waste it on wine?" Jenn said. "I could make you a scotch and soda."

"I want to eat supper with you and drink two glasses of wine," Jesse said.

"Maybe two," Jenn said.

They looked at each other. Both of them nodded.

Jenn poured some wine into his glass,

careful to make it a full glass, not to skimp as if she didn't trust him.

"And," Jenn said, "you should know that being too sexual with me is a great deal better than not being sexual enough."

Jesse smiled.

"I'll drink to that," he said.

ABOUT THE AUTHOR

ROBERT B. PARKER is the author of more than fifty books, including the bestsellers *Appaloosa* and *Cold Service*. He lives in Boston.